WESTERN **WP** PROMISES

WESTERN **WP** PROMISES

The Rancher's Runaway Princess

New York Times **Bestselling Author**
DONNA ALWARD

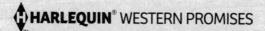

HARLEQUIN® WESTERN PROMISES

Recycling programs
for this product may
not exist in your area.

ISBN-13: 978-0-373-00337-2

The Rancher's Runaway Princess

First North American Publication 2009

Copyright © 2008 by Donna Alward

Printed in U.S.A.

Donna Alward is a busy wife and mother of three (two daughters and the family dog), and she believes hers is the best job in the world: a combination of stay-at-home mom and romance novelist. An avid reader since childhood, Donna has always made up her own stories. She completed her arts degree in English literature in 1994, but it wasn't until 2001 that she penned her first full-length novel and found herself hooked on writing romance. In 2006, she sold her first manuscript, and now writes warm, emotional stories for Harlequin.

In her home office in Nova Scotia, Donna loves being back on the east coast of Canada after nearly twelve years in Alberta, where her career began, writing about cowboys and the West. Donna's debut romance, *Hired by the Cowboy*, was awarded a Booksellers' Best Award in 2008 for Best Traditional Romance.

With the Atlantic Ocean only minutes from her doorstep, Donna has found a fresh take on life and promises even more great romances in the near future!

Donna loves to hear from readers. You can contact her through her website, donnaalward.com, or follow @DonnaAlward on Twitter.

Books by Donna Alward

Harlequin American Romance

The Cowboy's Christmas Family

Crooked Valley Ranch

The Cowboy's Christmas Gift
The Cowboy's Valentine
The Cowboy's Homecoming

Visit the Author Profile page
at Harlequin.com for more titles.

To Suzanne, who let me go first.

Chapter One

"In two hundred meters, turn left."

Lucy grinned lopsidedly in the direction of her GPS sitting on the dash. "Thank you, Bob," she replied with mock seriousness, looking up the long stretch of road for the intersection her "companion" kept insisting was approaching. The freedom—this wide-open space—was a revelation compared to how claustrophobic she'd felt lately.

"In one hundred meters, turn left."

She obeyed the monotone instruction and put on her turn signal. A small sign announced a numbered road. Thank goodness she'd been able to program in a waypoint for the Prairie Rose Ranch. Otherwise she would have kept driving the rented SUV through this fairly empty landscape for God knew how long. Not that she'd have minded; there was something comforting in the rolling green hills, their undulating curves broken only by random fences and trees.

She turned onto the road, only to discover after the first few seconds it had gravel instead of pavement. She rolled up the window against the dust curling up from her tires.

Prairie Rose Ranch was out in the middle of nowhere, just as Mr. Hamilton had said in his email. All that isolation and space had sounded wonderful to her ears after the scrutiny she'd experienced the past few months. She couldn't wait to get there, away from all the prying eyes and whispers from behind hands. In Canada there would be no expectations, even for a short time. At Prairie Rose she would just be Lucy Farnsworth.

Whoever that was.

She frowned as Bob announced he'd lost the satellite signal, grateful he'd got her this far. She was here to buy horses, to look into Hamilton's breeding program and negotiate stud fees. It was her first real responsibility and one she was more than equipped for. Granted, she couldn't shake the feeling that King Alexander was placating her, but it didn't matter. For the first time in a long time she felt in control of something. No one to tell her who she was or how to act.

And no one at the ranch need know who she really was. The last thing she needed—or wanted for that matter—was for everyone to look at her as if she had some invisible tiara perched on her head.

No, this was her chance to get away from all of the curiosity and assessments and do what she knew how to do. Nothing made sense to her anymore, but at least this trip, short as it was, might offer her a bit of a reprieve. Might offer her a chance to shake off the pervading sadness. She'd been thrown from one unimaginable situation into another without time to catch her breath. When Alexander had suggested this trip, she'd left a vapor trail that rivaled the one from the 777 she'd flown in.

On the left up ahead she caught sight of a group of buildings...big buildings. With a rumble of tires, the SUV ran over a Texas gate, leading her up to a graveled drive. A wood and iron arch embraced the entrance, and she knew she was in the right place when she looked up and saw a uniquely shaped iron rose in the centre. Bob came back to life and announced she was arriving at her destination, but she reached over blindly and shut the unit off.

Her eyes assessed the ranch as she drove slowly up the long, straight lane. It was neat, well kept, with a rambling two-story farmhouse hidden behind a long barn and corral. The immediate fences were in good repair and freshly painted; nothing seemed out of place. So far so good.

The land here was different from where she'd grown up, yet somewhat the same, and very different from the sun-baked countryside in Marazur. The sky here was broad and robin's-egg blue, in contrast to the piercing blue of the Mediterranean sky. Horses dotted the landscape, up a hill and beyond, grazing on rich grass, reminding her of her childhood home in Virginia. It was comforting and unsettling at the same time. It was what she knew. Yet everything she thought she knew about herself had been a lie, and she wanted to run away even as the ranch beckoned to her. Maybe this wasn't such a good idea after all.

Nothing made sense, and that was the *only* consistent thing these days.

She pulled in next to a white truck with the same Prairie Rose brand painted on the side, got out and shut the door. The polite thing to do would be to introduce herself at the house, she supposed. But then what? The west wind buffeted her curls about her face and she pushed them aside. The wind carried with it the sound of voices, coming from the open sliding door of the barn. Thankful she'd changed clothing before the drive, she straightened her T-shirt. At least someone in the barn could point her in the right direction.

Lucy heard the man before she saw him, his voice a low, warm rumble as he spoke. Her sneakers made soft padding noises on the concrete floor; for a moment she stopped and closed her eyes, drinking in the mellow smell of hay and straw and the warm pungency of horse, the one true thing that she associated with home. Perhaps that was what kept her going during all the dark days and uncertainty. The one constant she'd always had. The one place where she'd always belonged, no matter where she was. In a barn with the horses.

She knew it, and resented it. Resented that

it was the only thing she seemed to have left. The male voice said something else, punctuated like a question. He was answered by a distinctly female voice, who laughed a little, though Lucy couldn't make out what they were saying. She paused, wondering again if she should have made herself known at the house first. She didn't want to intrude. But she turned a corner and suddenly two pairs of legs were before her and she couldn't pretend now that she hadn't come in.

He...the owner of the voice...stood upright, his weight planted squarely over his booted feet. One hand was resting on the withers of a splendid-looking chestnut mare. Lucy was first aware of his considerable height. Which made her realize how long his legs were in his faded jeans. Which led to his T-shirt. And how the worn cotton emphasized an impressively broad chest.

Color flooded her cheeks. Her assessment had taken all of two seconds, but it was complete, right down to the hot rush of appreciation.

"Can I help you?"

Lucy swallowed against the spit pooling in her mouth. She shot out her hand. "Lucy Farnsworth." *Please, please let him not be*

Brody Hamilton, she prayed silently, with her hand suspended in midair. It wasn't possible that the man she'd just been caught blatantly staring at was the man she'd been sent here to broker deals with.

At her revelation he removed his hat, revealing a dark head and even darker eyes that crinkled at the corners with good humor. Her heart thumped at the courtesy...it was natural, not a put-on gesture, she was sure. He smiled as he stepped forward and took her small hand in his large one. "I beg your pardon, Miss Farnsworth. I'm Brody Hamilton. You made good time."

So this *was* Hamilton. So much for answered prayer. His fingers wrapped around hers and her tummy turned over.

Prairie Rose was a reputable operation. She'd expected the owner to be older. Certainly more plain looking, like most of the ranchers she'd grown up knowing. She hadn't expected him to be tall and sexy and all of what, thirty? Thirty-five? She kept the polite smile glued to her face, but inside she was growling to herself. Acting like a blushing schoolgirl. She was beyond that, wasn't she? And she was here to do a job, for Pete's sake!

"My flight was a little early."

She withdrew her hand, giving it a small tug. His fingers were warm and callused and had covered hers completely. She'd enjoyed the sensation, too much. Knowing it made her uncomfortable. There was no reason on earth why a single handshake should cause all this commotion within her.

It's just a physical reaction, she told herself. He *was* a fine-looking man, there was no sense denying it. She'd always admired that rugged, large, capable type, and he certainly fit that category. Any woman would have reacted the same way.

"This is my farrier, Martha," he introduced the woman holding the halter of the mare. Martha was taller than Lucy, sturdy, with slightly graying hair and was at least forty-five.

"You're from Marazur," Martha announced, releasing the halter and shaking Lucy's hand. "The Navarro family is renowned for their royal stables. It's a pleasure."

Why Lucy felt a tiny shaft of pride at that statement she had no idea. She'd been in Marazur all of two months and certainly couldn't take any credit for the stock owned by His Highness. It wasn't as if she belonged there or anything. Alexander had merely indulged her by letting her potter around; she'd heard him telling his eldest son that very thing. He'd let her come on this trip just for appearances. He hadn't known what to do with her and this was easy. But that didn't matter. She was here now, and she would surprise them all by making the visit a success. Hamilton didn't know who she was. He wouldn't suspect her credibility, and she'd make sure it stayed that way.

"Brody's been telling me about you coming," Martha continued.

"It's not every day we get to do business with a royal family," Brody admitted, smiling down at her. It was slightly crooked, and her heart gave another traitorous thump.

Brody Hamilton was a charmer. With the realization of it, Lucy immediately felt better. Charm she could deal with. Charm only went so far, like good looks. It was blood that would tell. And unlike her mother, she wasn't going to fall for a wink and a smile. His would be wiped off his face soon enough, when he realized she actually knew what she was doing.

"Yes, well, I'm far more interested in the stock." She moved ahead and rubbed her hand on the hide just above the mare's nose.

She closed her eyes briefly, smiling at the way the mare rubbed into her hand, enjoying the attention. "What's up with you, lovely? Hmm?"

"A bruise, nothing more. She stumbled during a trail ride yesterday."

"Trail ride?"

"We do give them now and then, a couple of hours and most people have had their fill of horseback. It keeps some of the older stock exercised. Besides…it's fun. Martha assures me a day or so in her box and this girl'll be right as rain." He rubbed the mare's neck as he said it.

There was that crooked grin again, accompanied by the crinkled corners of his eyes that seemed to be teasing. She turned away from him.

"And this beautiful girl is what—" she made a cursory examination "—sixteen? Seventeen?"

"Sixteen." Brody's smile had faded slightly.

Lucy ran her hand down the gleaming neck, her gaze taking in the shape of the ears, the forehead, the wide-set eyes. There was no doubt about it. She'd know that head anywhere. A smile flirted with her lips. What a pleasant surprise.

"Which would make her…one of Pretty Colleen's," she announced triumphantly. His flirtatious grin wouldn't get far with her, and she would make sure he knew it. She knew her business, and he needed to know that. She wasn't just an emissary sent to broker a deal.

Brody's smile disappeared completely. He stared at Miss Farnsworth, trying to puzzle her out. How on earth could she tell that? He'd bought Pretty Piece from a farm in Tennessee when she was eight…one of his first purchases on his own. This little moppet with the red curls, Lucy, she would have been a child when Pretty foaled. And she was from Marazur. The Mediterranean was a long way from backroads Alberta. Yet her accent didn't bear it out. She wasn't native to Marazur. He was as certain of that as he was that Pretty Piece was indeed of Pretty Colleen. A fact she couldn't have known before today, not unless she'd had a look at his records.

Who was Lucy Farnsworth? His brows snapped together. There was more to her than first appeared. He wondered how much more.

"How did you know?"

"It's her head. Looks just like her mum."

Brody shook his head while Martha laughed. "Congratulations, Miss Farnsworth.

I think you've rendered him speechless. Quite a feat, because most of the time he has *something* to say."

"Martha!" Brody frowned. Never mind that at one point, Martha had been his babysitter and had changed his diapers.

Martha reached down for her bag. "Oh, pipe down, Junior. The girl knows her stuff, that's all. I'll be back in a few days to check on the mare."

She blustered out leaving Brody and Lucy in the gap, each with a hand on Pretty.

Somewhere outside a soft whicker echoed.

"I'll admit, Miss Farnsworth, you surprised me just now." He put his hat back on his head.

"I have that effect on people."

"Maybe sometime you'd care to explain that." He let a little humor sneak into his voice; she piqued his curiosity plain and simple. She'd clearly been around the industry a long time. Despite her youth, she seemed knowledgeable. And her accent was Stateside. Southeast somewhere, he gathered. "Where are you from, anyway?"

For a moment their eyes clashed and he sensed she was deciding how to answer what should have been a simple question. He tried a smile, inviting her to speak. To his surprise her eyes immediately cooled and her lips thinned.

"You must have work to do," she offered stiffly.

"There's always work, but I expect you know that." She didn't want to answer. He wondered why, but there'd be time to get that information. She was supposed to stay several days.

"I'll just—" She swallowed, let the sentence hang.

"You've had a long flight and drive. You probably want to rest. I'll take you up to the house."

"You said you had work."

He angled his head slightly. He couldn't quite figure out Lucy Farnsworth. She was younger than he'd expected, especially to be so involved with such a renowned stable. It was clear she'd been sent because she could do the job. He wasn't sure why, but he'd expected someone taller, with dark hair and a remote manner.

The only thing that bore out his expectations was the manner. There could be no mistaking the coolness, the only warmth she'd shown was in the caresses she'd spared

Pretty. But tall and elegant she was not. She was barely up to his shoulder, and her hair was a tangle of gingery ringlets that flirted with her cheekbones until she tucked them behind her ears.

"I do, but that doesn't mean I can't get you settled in the house first."

Lucy looked away from him, as if what she was going to say next was so uncomfortable she couldn't meet his eyes. She instead looked Pretty in the eyes and scratched between the mare's ears. "I assumed I'd be in a guest house."

"We don't have a guest house, but then there's no need. There's more than enough room." He had a fleeting thought of running into her in the hall at sunrise, her curls in disarray and her cheeks still pink from the warmth of her bed....

Where the hell had that come from?

"I don't mean to impose on you, Mr. Hamilton. I can stay at the hotel in the town I drove through. What was it called... Larch something or other?"

"Larch Valley, and it's a twenty-minute drive." Perhaps not a bad idea, come to think of it, but the agreement had been made that he'd provide accommodation. He didn't want it said that he didn't provide proper hospitality. This was an important deal. And part of that was providing all that the ranch had to offer.

"That's a short commute in most places." Her voice interrupted him again.

Brody walked to a nearby hook and grabbed a lead, snapping it on to the mare's halter. "If you're more comfortable there, I understand. I'm sorry the arrangements weren't made clear. But why drive it if you don't have to?"

"I don't know…"

He sensed her hesitation and pressed on. "At least stay for dinner. If Mrs. Polcyk can't convince you with her roast chicken…"

He let the thought trail off. Why was he insisting, anyway? The hotel back in town wasn't *that* bad. It had its good points—it was clean.

But he'd given his word to King Alexander. That his representative would be shown every hospitality. That whoever was sent would be received as an honored guest. He just hadn't expected it to be a sharp-tongued slip of a girl.

Brody didn't do well with girls. At least not beyond sharing a dance on a Saturday night.

Especially one he tried to charm with a smile and who saw clear through it.

"I don't want to be in your way."

"The day starts early here, and sometimes finishes late. It's much more convenient, but of course, it's whatever makes you most comfortable. You are our guest, Miss Farnsworth. I'll leave it up to you."

Brody tried very hard not to wrinkle his brow. He'd seen her eyes when she'd first stepped into the corridor. He and Martha had taken her by surprise, and for a tiny moment Miss Farnsworth had looked small and vulnerable. Her eyes had gone a little wide and then darkened with a whole lot of assessment. She probably didn't even realize it but she'd bitten down on her lip and he'd been tempted to laugh. A cute little thing, he'd thought. A little out of her element, pretty and fresh, and he'd wanted to make her blush.

But then he'd realized who she was. A representative sent to assess his stock. A woman who knew horses, supposedly better than most men he knew. His Highness had said so when he called. Brody couldn't dispute that fact…it took a keen eye to identify an offspring by its parent, and the way she touched Pretty was confident and kind. For some reason Lucy Farnsworth was willing to sacrifice comfort for isolation. Why?

Lucy stepped away from the horse and backed up a few steps. Hamilton was right. She'd known the agreement included accommodation, and to drive to and from town when she didn't have to didn't make sense. The only reason not to stay here—the only one—was that she already felt awkward around Brody. Which was foolish.

Here she was representing the royal family of Marazur and she was astute enough to know that staying in town would be a deliberate snub against her host. And in the days ahead she might want Brody in good humor during negotiations.

"Of course the house will be lovely. I just don't want to be an inconvenience to you."

"You won't be, I assure you. The house was built for a large family and is a little lonely with only two in it.

"Two?" She had a fleeting thought of a wife and, for one ridiculous moment, felt more awkward than ever.

"Me, and Mrs. Polcyk. She's the housekeeper and cook. She's been looking forward to having someone else to do for, other than grumpy old me."

She looked up into his eyes—dark like the warm molasses her mother used to put on her bread. Right now he didn't look grumpy *or* old. The tummy-turning deliciousness was back, helped along by a breathlessness so foreign to her she didn't recognize it at first.

Brody Hamilton was sex on a stick, from his delicious eyes to his long legs to his manner that somehow managed to convey energy *and* a lazy ease. There was no escaping the facts; the only thing she could control was her reaction.

She took a deep breath and pasted on her polite-yet-distant royal smile…the one and only aspect of her new life she'd mastered. She remembered how big the house was and nodded. She probably wouldn't even run into Brody most of the time. "I appreciate it."

"Let me finish up with Pretty and I'll take you up. You can have a look around if you want."

"I'll do that."

He led the horse away, and Lucy watched them depart down the corridor, boots and hooves echoing through the quiet space. His faded jeans fit him as if they were made for him, the dark T-shirt emphasizing his broad shoulders. The black brim of his cowboy hat shaded his neck.

She squared her shoulders and set her jaw. Life had been full of enough complications lately. And she'd be damned if she'd let Brody Hamilton be another one.

Chapter Two

Lucy perched on a wooden stool, sipped on a cup of strong, rich coffee and came to two important conclusions.

Number one, Brody Hamilton ran a good ship. Everything was kept in tip-top shape, and from what she'd seen, that extended to his horses. This was a good thing. You could tell a lot about a man's stock by the state of the rest of the farm. Prairie Rose was neat, tidy and organized. Brody Hamilton paid attention.

And number two, Mrs. Polcyk ran the house. Full stop.

Lucy smiled into her mug, remembering

how the housekeeper had put Brody firmly into his place. Brody had introduced her to the round, apple-cheeked woman who had instantly bustled her inside. Mrs. Polcyk had then ordered Brody to bring up Lucy's things, and he'd obeyed without batting a single one of his obscenely long eyelashes. He'd done it without a grimace or an eye roll but with an innate respect and acceptance of her, and Lucy liked that about him as well.

Lucy, on the other hand, was ushered through to the kitchen where she was now watching Mrs. Polcyk take some sort of pastry out of the oven. The room smelled of coffee grounds and cinnamon and fruit.

All of it filled her with such a sense of homesickness she thought she might cry. She missed afternoons like this. Tea in the drawing room was not quite the same as hot coffee and cookies in the kitchen.

"Your bags are in your room."

Brody's rich voice came from behind her, and she swallowed coffee and the tears that had gathered in her throat. She hadn't realized that coming here would hurt her so much. Hadn't realized that it would remind her of a place where she no longer belonged. And it was clear Brody took all that for granted. She wondered if he realized how lucky he was.

But she couldn't say any of that, of course. She put the smile back in its place and spun on the stool to face him. "Thank you."

"My pleasure."

He took a few long steps until he was at the stool next to her. He hardly had to move at all to perch on its seat and Lucy was reminded again how very tall he was. His voice was deep and full of teasing as he leaned forward, egging on Mrs. Polcyk. "If you tell me that's cherry strudel, I'm yours forever, Mrs. P."

She flapped a hand in his direction, but pulled a thick white mug out of a cupboard and poured him a cup of coffee.

Lucy felt his eyes on her and she refused to meet them again. If she did he'd see the tears that still glimmered there, and the last thing she needed was for him to see her vulnerable. And with him watching her so intently, there wasn't an opportunity for her to wipe them away. She opened her eyes as wide as she could, willing the moisture to evaporate. She'd thought of this trip as a chance to escape. Instead, the grief she'd tamped down for the last months rose up, leaving her raw and breathless.

For a few minutes they sipped in silence. He seemed to be waiting for her to speak, and she couldn't come up with anything to talk about. Her personal life was strictly off-limits. For one, she would fall apart, and for another, he would treat her differently, and that was the last thing she wanted. Maybe it was jet lag, because she knew she should ask him about Prairie Rose and his breeding program and hundreds of other relevant questions. Instead her brain was riddled with personal questions. Why was he the only one here? Did he run this place completely on his own? How was Mrs. Polcyk related to him? But for her to ask him those questions would be opening herself up to ones of a similar nature, and she couldn't have that.

Instead she stared into her coffee cup, fighting off memories and twisting her lips. It had to be fatigue, nothing else made sense. Certainly the feeling of resentment that was bubbling underneath all the other emotions didn't add up. He was teasing and comfortable. And she knew he had no idea how he was taking his situation for granted. No one ever did until they'd lost and then they were left with regrets. She'd bet any money that Brody didn't have regrets.

At least that made it easier for her to dislike him. Disliking him was vastly easier than liking. If she didn't like him, she wouldn't be tempted to reveal more than she should.

"Miss Farnsworth?"

She chanced a look up. He was looking at her over the rim of his cup, his eyes serious. "We've got plenty of time to talk business. If you're tired, you don't need to put up a good front. The jet lag alone has got to be killing you."

He was giving her an excuse; being kind to a guest. And it would be a good opportunity for her to create more distance between them. She should take it. Yet the thought of facing an empty, unfamiliar room wasn't that attractive. She'd spent enough time alone lately.

"You can start by calling me Lucy." The staff in Marazur reluctantly called her Miss Farnsworth after she'd dressed them down for using her official title. She couldn't abide the "ma'am" they'd come out with on her first day, either. Even "Miss Farnsworth" made her feel like a stranger; she was used to her stable mates calling, "Hey, Luce" down the corridor. But she hadn't been able to convince the staff to call her Lucy. She didn't want to be Miss anything or Princess anyone. She wanted to be Lucy. Maybe if Brody would call her by her name she wouldn't feel like such a fraud.

"I like your house," she offered, an attempt at civility. "It's very...homey."

Something dark flitted through his eyes even though his tone was teasing as he responded, "As the head of King Alexander's stables, I expect you're used to finer accommodations."

"Not at all. It's not like I grew up in the palace." That much was true. She hadn't laid eyes on Marazur until a few short months ago. And arriving at the palace had been a shock. She'd grown up in a very modest middle-class neighborhood. She was used to worn furniture and chipped dishes, not antique settees and fine china. She was torn jeans and T-shirts; Marazur was linen and lace. "I had a typical middle-class upbringing, you might say. I'm just...ordinary," she conceded.

"How *did* you get the job, anyway? You're awfully young."

"Too young?" She bristled, familiar with the refrain. It was easier to do battle on the age front than admit she was there because of Daddy.

"Obviously not. I get the feeling you know exactly what you're doing."

He didn't make it sound like a compliment, but it was wrapped in politeness so it was hard to tell.

"I grew up around quarter horses, and I…" She paused, considered. She didn't want him to know. He couldn't know. There would be no more coffee breaks in the kitchen, and she'd missed them desperately. Even if southern Alberta was vastly different from Virginia, this kitchen held the same feel as the one she remembered, and she was hungry for those feelings again, no matter how bittersweet. Mrs. Polcyk refilled her cup, and the scent of the brew drew her back to the smell of strong coffee in the office at Trembling Oak; to the tin of cookies that had always seemed to make its way to the scarred wooden table. These were the feelings of home.

She didn't want to be treated any differently. As long as he thought of her as Lucy, she could pretend she'd escaped, even for a little while. If he knew who she was, he wouldn't take her seriously. And the truth was she needed him to believe in her competence. Needed him to know she was fully capable of doing this job.

"It was a case of knowing someone who knew someone, that was all."

Brody's jaw tightened. First she'd called his house "homey" as if she couldn't come up with a better word. Then she'd all but admitted she'd got her job by knowing someone. *Nepotism.* He despised the word. It reminded him of someone else. Someone who'd once considered Prairie Rose Ranch a little too rustic for her taste. His fingers tightened around the handle of his cup.

Mrs. Polcyk put plates of warm strudel in front of them and bustled away to the refrigerator. Brody examined the square and told himself to forget it. It didn't matter who or what Lucy Farnsworth was. She was not Lisa, and all that mattered was concluding their business. Being allied to the House of Navarro and King Alexander was what was important. It would mean great things for the ranch and the breeding program he'd worked so hard to improve since taking over.

Brody cut a corner off with his fork and popped the buttery pastry into his mouth. "Cherry. God bless her." He sighed with appreciation.

Lucy smiled thinly, almost as if she were unaccustomed to it. What he really wanted to know was more about King Alexander and his plans. Allying himself to one of the greatest stables in Europe would be a huge coup. He'd be able to grow his breeding program the way he wanted, really put Prairie Rose on the map. He owed that to his father. He owed it to himself, and to Mrs. Polcyk.

"What's it like? Working for someone so high profile?"

Lucy picked up her own fork to hide her surprise. Briefly she'd sensed Hamilton's withdrawal and got the uneasy feeling he was somehow mad at her. Now he was asking questions. Prying veiled in small talk. If he really wanted to know about her, all he'd have to do was a bit of navigating online and he'd get the whole story. She would have to give him enough to keep him from doing that, and not enough to let the cat out of the bag.

She was in such a quandary that she took a second bite of strudel before answering, pressing the buttery layers with her tongue, letting them melt. She'd been around a lot of livestock men in her life, and conversation was usually not one of their finer points. She had to acknowledge that he was making an effort, and for the sake of amicability, she considered how to answer.

Working for King Alexander was stifling at times, knowing why she was there in the first place. Being told she belonged there, when she knew she didn't. Yet it was glorious at others, like when she got to go riding through the fields without asking permission. Being able to hand pick her own mount, with no restrictions. That little slice of freedom was all that had kept her sane.

She couldn't reveal any of that to Hamilton, not if she wanted him to respect her capabilities. Not if she wanted him to see her as more than Daddy's girl flirting around with the horsies. She knew ranchers. Knew that was exactly what he'd think.

She squared her shoulders and forced a smile.

"His Highness has fine stables and the best in facilities and equipment. His tack room alone is half the size of your barn, all of it gleaming and smelling of rich leather. Navarro horses are in demand all over Europe, from riding horses for the privileged to show jumpers to racing stock. His staff is dedicated and knowledgeable. It's a manager's dream come true."

"But?"

She put down her fork slowly, met his eyes while pursing her lips in puzzlement. "What do you mean, 'but'?"

"But what are you leaving out?"

"Nothing. It's a great operation."

"Then why aren't you meeting my eyes when you tell me about it?"

"I beg your pardon?" She felt color rise in her cheeks and took a deliberate sip of her cooling coffee. She'd been deliberately vague, and now he was calling her on it. She never had been good at hiding her feelings. Her mother always said Lucy had no face for poker and that Lucy had come by it honestly, as she hadn't had one, either. It had been years before Lucy understood what she'd really meant.

"You're avoiding looking at me. My mother always said that was a sign of a liar."

She bristled. An hour. She'd known him barely an hour and he was calling her a liar! The mug came down smartly on the countertop. He couldn't know who she really was. And if he did, pretending he didn't was downright rude. Mrs. Polcyk looked over, then calmly went back to cutting vegetables.

"Are you accusing me of something?"

"Of course not. I'm just wondering what you're not saying. This is my operation and my stock you're looking at. I don't get to travel to Marazur to check things out first. And when I get a sense that there's more to a story, I want to know before I sign anything on a dotted line."

She stood up from her stool. Dammit, even sitting he was slightly taller than she was. "You're insinuating that I'm withholding something about the Navarro stables. I don't appreciate that. The hotel is looking better and better. Navarro stables doesn't need Prairie Rose Ranch, not as much as..." She looked around her and then back into his face, lifting her chin. "Not as much as you need Navarro. You aren't the only stud operation in the world."

The anger felt good, releasing. Even if she knew provoking him would be a tactical mistake.

His eyes glinted like dark shards. "Perhaps not. But I was under the impression King Alexander wanted the best."

She met his gaze, admiring his confidence despite how annoying it was.

"And you're the best, I suppose."

"You wouldn't have come all this way if I weren't."

Her lips thinned. He had her to rights there. She *had* come a long way, and it was all to do with Hamilton's Ahab. That horse was the main reason she was here, as well as having the discretion to negotiate further stud fees and even add to Navarro with Prairie Rose stock.

"You're very sure of yourself."

"Don't get all in a dander over it. You described the stables like a brochure would, that's all. I'm just curious to know more. I like to know who I'm dealing with."

His implacable calm fueled her temper. Who was he to question the integrity of Navarro? She shoved her hands in her pockets to keep them from fidgeting. She knew she shouldn't rise to the bait but with the exhaustion and surprising emotionalism, she seemed incapable of ignoring it. "All you need to know is that I'm here to do a job. A job I'm more than qualified to do. Nothing else is up for discussion."

She spun to walk away, but his voice stopped her.

"Run away, then."

Everything inside her froze.

Run away? Her breath caught at his casual tone. If only she could. If only she could run away from what her life had become. She was so sick of everyone telling her how wonderfully things had turned out in the end. It didn't feel that way *at all*. Everything, *everything* she thought she'd known had been taken away with one conversation. Life had changed irrevocably, and right now all she could see was what she'd lost along the way.

Her job. Her home. Her mother.

Yes, she wished she could run away. But instead she was back to trying to prove herself and find *something* to anchor her again so she wouldn't feel as if she were drifting in this endless sea of loss and grief. And that something was her job at the stables, and her task was clear: the breeding program here at Prairie Rose.

And that meant that in the present she had to somehow deal with Brody Hamilton.

She turned and looked at him, sitting there, his black eyes watching her keenly, waiting for a response. Waiting as if he could see through every wall she'd built around herself and knew what she was hiding on the inside.

And for one brief, irrational moment she did want to run. Not away, but into the circle of his arms. They looked like strong arms, arms a woman could get lost in and forget the rest of the world existed. For months now she'd been standing on her own and she was tired. Tired of feeling she had to apologize for not being happy. Tired of pretending, when all she wanted was life back the way she'd had it. Tired of knowing even the past she'd thought secure had been based on a lie. For a few moments she wondered what it would be like to rest her head on his strong shoulder and just *be*. To let someone carry the weight for a while.

She swallowed. This was ridiculous. She hardly knew him and what she did know she resented. It had to be exhaustion, it was the only reason that made sense to her. There was no other reason for her to feel drawn to Brody Hamilton. None at all.

Looking at him…he just knew where he belonged. He was solid and steady, and he *fit* in a way she never had.

That was reason enough to resist the urge to step into his arms. Reason enough to resent him for all he had and the fact that he probably didn't even know it. The thought of stepping into his embrace was laughable. This was a man who'd just questioned her integrity. She should be taking him down a peg. Instead she was bone tired of all of it. Her gaze dropped to his lips, and something intimate curled through her core. She mentally took a step backward.

"It's hardly productive for us to argue," she said, as icily as she could muster. "I believe you were right about the jet lag. I'm not myself. If you'll excuse me… I'm sure by tomorrow I'll be squared away and ready to get to work."

His eyes revealed nothing.

"Of course." The words were cold with empty manners.

"I'll take you up, dear." Mrs. Polcyk came around the corner with a gentle smile. Lucy turned her back on Brody again, forcing yet another smile for the kindly housekeeper. She could still sense his dark eyes on her, and they made her feel naked.

"You'll be wanting a nice hot bath, and a good meal—dinner's not far off."

What Lucy wanted was to disappear for the rest of the night, but she couldn't help but be comforted by the motherly insistence that somehow food would make everything right.

"That sounds wonderful."

She followed Mrs. Polcyk to the stairs but

turned back at the last moment, displaying some sense of good manners her mum had instilled in her.

"I'll see you at dinner, Mr. Hamilton."

"Yes'm."

The housekeeper led her to the last room along the hall; a large bedroom with a window facing due west. "The bathroom is next door," Lucy heard, though her gaze was caught by the view of the mountains hovering in the distance. She'd seen them on the highway coming south from Calgary, but since turning east at Larch Valley, they'd slid from view. Now from the second floor window they jutted, gray, dark teeth, up to the hazy blue sky.

"Can you always see the mountains from here?" Lucy spun toward Mrs. Polcyk, who was standing with her hand on the doorknob.

"Most clear days. Wait'll you see the view from Wade's Butte."

"Wade's Butte?" Lucy couldn't recall seeing that on her map.

"Get Brody to take you out. It's probably a couple of hours ride, just on the edge of the ranch land."

"The name's not familiar."

"'Course not. You won't find it on any map,

though most from around here know it right enough. It just sort of got named that, after Brody's granddad."

Mrs. Polcyk aimed a bright smile. "You just go relax now, and put on your eatin' legs. I made roast chicken tonight and there's peach cobbler for dessert. Cally brought back two cases from BC last week."

Lucy had no idea who Cally was and wasn't quite sure what "BC" was, but peach cobbler sounded heavenly. "I'm looking forward to it," she replied, with as much warmth as she could muster.

Mrs. Polcyk shut the door and left Lucy alone.

She looked around the room. It was different from any place she'd ever stayed. The floor looked like original hardwood, polished within an inch of its life, and the furniture gleamed from a fresh cleaning. The spread on the bed was homemade, a brilliant cacophony of bright colors and fabrics that made a patchwork pattern of flowers. Fresh flowers sat in a vase on the side table. Lucy went over and dipped her nose to sniff at a nasturtium. These weren't purchased at any store. These had been cut from a garden, today. For her.

The deliberate welcome touched her, despite Brody's gruff manner. He'd all but accused her of lying, but he'd been right. Perhaps that was what had annoyed her so much. It would be a cold day in hell before she would admit it.

She took out fresh clothing and wandered next door to the bathroom, delighted to find a small basket of little toiletries on the vanity next to a pile of fluffy towels. She put the plug in the tub and added some salts, breathing in the fragrant steam. Summertime or not, after a full day's travel added in with the time difference, a hot bath sounded like luxury itself.

An hour later, refreshed and dressed with her damp curls framing her face, she made her way back downstairs to dinner.

Brody was in the kitchen. And he was mashing potatoes.

Lucy stopped at the bottom of the stairs, watching the scene without being noticed. His hat was off, his dark hair lying in fine whorls around his skull, his dark T-shirt clinging to his wide shoulders with each push of the masher. Behind him Mrs. Polcyk wielded a set of electric beaters, whipping cream in a clear, cold bowl. Lucy's mouth went dry at the sight of his muscles flexing as he lifted the huge jug of milk and dumped some into the pot, scooped up some butter on a spoon and stirred it all together with a sure hand.

She really had been without a date too long. Because the sight of big Brody Hamilton whipping potatoes was doing things to her insides that she hadn't felt in a very long time. He was *tempting*. So physically powerful that her body betrayed her, and when he smiled at Mrs. Polcyk, a dimple popped in his left cheek.

Oh, my.

He reached over Mrs. Polcyk's head for a serving bowl and muttered something; Lucy nearly laughed out loud as he then skillfully dodged an errant female elbow that came flying his way.

She'd had time to think while in the bath and she knew that Brody had been right. She had been deliberately hiding something and it was natural he'd be suspicious. There was no way for him to know that she'd rather have her old life back than be ensconced at some cold stone palace in Europe. She'd also realized she needed to volunteer information about the stables and not herself. It was all a matter of slanting the focus to put him at ease.

She'd made a promise, and she wouldn't go back on it. Even if it was the last thing she'd wanted.

Brody put the bowl on the table and turned, spying her standing by the stairway. His happy, unguarded look faded as he saw her, and she wondered why it was he disliked her so much already. "Dinner's on," he said blandly.

Mrs. Polcyk took a platter of chicken to the table, followed by vegetables and a boat of golden gravy. "Please sit down, Lucy," she invited.

Lucy took the chair at the end; for some reason it seemed like the vacant spot. Brody took the other end while the housekeeper perched herself in the middle.

Mrs. Polcyk dipped her grayed head and to Lucy's surprise began a prayer in a language she didn't understand.

When it was over Lucy lifted her head and met Brody's eyes. Something warm passed between them, something that spoke of a unity and recognition even though they were strangers from different lives.

And Lucy knew she had to back away from it as fast as she could. Nothing good could come of it. She couldn't get close to Brody Hamilton.

She couldn't allow herself to get close to anyone.

Chapter Three

Brody woke to moonlight tracing a pale line along his bedroom wall. He rolled to his back, rubbing a hand over the stubble on his face.

He'd been dreaming of her. Dreaming of her corkscrew hair falling over his hands the moment before he pressed his mouth to her defiant lips.

He raised up on to his elbows, shaking his head a bit in the dark. He wasn't a man prone to dreams, especially about women he'd just met. But something about Lucy pushed his buttons. She was stubborn and abrasive, and damned smart if he were any judge at all.

Carrying a chip on her shoulder the size of Marazur.

Yet there was something behind it. Something he couldn't quite put his finger on. It was in the way she'd looked at him just before dinner tonight; the way their eyes had met after Mrs. P.'s saying of grace. She could be as icy as she pleased, but there was *something* about her that called to him.

And he would ignore that call. Her life was vastly different from his, and there was no way he'd forget it. Once burned... Well, that had been enough for him.

It was crazy, thinking about her this way. It was ridiculous to even admit to himself that he felt a physical attraction to her. It'd come plain out of nowhere and had hit him square in the gut. He'd disputed it to himself earlier but there was no arguing with the dream.

He rose from the bed and moved to the open window. Cool, crisp air fluttered over his skin. The hot, dry breezes of July nights were gone; in their place were the cold, clear nights of August, chill and full of stars. The air rushed in through the screen and he let it clear his head.

Then he saw the light.

The windows at the front end of the barn

gleamed in the inky blackness. And he was positive he'd turned everything out before going to bed.

He pulled on his jeans in brisk, quiet movements. He carried his boots in his hands and crept down the stairs, checking his watch as he went. The luminescent hands gleamed at the two and the four—two-twenty. When he got to the door he saw Mrs. P.'s jacket hung precisely beside his denim one. He snagged the latter, shoved his arms in the sleeves and slid out the door into the brisk night air.

He crept toward the barn door, which was opened a few feet, letting out a rhombus-shaped slice of yellow light. A quiet shuffle sounded; someone was definitely inside. He turned back toward the house for a moment, suspicion forming in his mind. Lucy's room was dark, no light from the bedroom windows at the west end of the house. As another shuffle sounded, he turned again to the barn.

She'd arrived today and now someone was in his barns in the middle of the night. Coincidence? He didn't think so.

What was she up to? What could she possibly be looking for? Brody exhaled slowly. All important records were locked in the office up at the house. And she likely knew that. Which meant…

Which meant she was sneaking around his horses. Tampering, sabotage—whatever she was doing he was going to put a stop to it right now.

He squeezed through the opening between door and wall and slowly made his way through the shadows, toward the office. A light was on inside, but another shuffle told him that whoever had turned it on was no longer inside. Instead the sound came from a stall on the right. He held his breath…there was the sound again, followed by the hollow echo of shifting hooves. Pretty's box. The horse she'd met earlier. His heart gave a heavy thump.

Brody squared his shoulders, took four silent, long strides that took him to the stall door.

It, too, was open.

He slid it open wider, bracing himself for who or what he'd find, inhaling and filling the doorway so whoever was inside would have to go through him first.

A woman's voice stopped him. "It's not fair" he heard over the sound of shaky breaths. "You're the princess, Pretty. Not me."

Not fair. The words seemed to bounce around in his head as his heart clubbed. If she was in there to hurt Pretty…

He leaped into the stall. And stopped at the sight of wide brown eyes staring up at him in shock and fear, still clinging to Pretty's mane and standing close to her withers.

Brody's mouth opened but he had nothing to say for the first few seconds. The lashes above her eyes were wet with tears, and as he watched in fascinated horror, one slid down over her pale cheek and dropped off her jaw into the straw by her feet. Her lips were puffy, the way he'd imagined them being after he'd kissed them in his dream, soft and fragile. And her fingers were twined in Pretty's mane as the chestnut stood quietly at her side.

"What in the world are you doing?"

"I… I, uh, it was…" Lucy stammered, a guilty flush adding to her already red and chapped cheeks.

"Eloquent." He blocked the doorway, determined to get answers and equally determined not to let her tears influence the conversation. Pretty was a valuable mare and more than that, she was his. Nope, Miss Farnsworth had some explaining to do. And fast.

"I came to be alone." She shot the words

out all in one go, attempting a defiance that fell completely flat.

"So you're sneaking around in the middle of the night? What are you really after? If you're here to harm my horses…" He took a menacing step. "No king will protect you here, Miss Farnsworth."

She gawped at him with what looked like disbelief. Good, he thought. Calling her out might just get him some answers. She blinked back the remaining tears, and his shoulders relaxed a little. Relief. He didn't deal well with tears and histrionics.

"After? You think I'm after something?"

"Are you kidding? You arrive today and your first night here I find you snooping around my stock while you're supposed to be asleep? What would you think?"

He watched, utterly entranced as she swallowed, casting her eyes on her feet. She was caught. Guilt was written all over her pink cheeks.

"I'm sorry. Of course you would think that. I…please believe me, Mr. Hamilton. I had no…untoward intentions by coming here tonight."

"Then, why are you here?"

Stoically she looked away, focused on

Pretty's neck, smoothing her hand over the gleaming hide.

"Isn't it obvious?"

"Not exactly. Beyond that you're upset." He stepped another foot forward, shortening the distance between them. He would look in her eyes. Then he'd know for sure if she was telling the truth. "That's a given."

Her lower lip trembled until she bit it, worrying it with her teeth. Brody stopped, shoved his hands in his pockets.

"I came here to be alone. To…to have a cry out, okay? I never meant to disturb you."

A stranger was in his barn in the middle of the night bawling all over one of his horses. This was a first. His brows knit together. Granted, he'd been short with her a few times today. But she'd gone toe-to-toe with him and he'd respected that. He hadn't gotten the impression she was the weepy sort.

But she was definitely weepy now, and he had to admit her story rang true. Those tears hadn't been manufactured when he'd burst through the stall door. And he remembered doing handkerchief duty for Lisa and stepped backward. He'd done his time with crying females and didn't care to again.

"Mornin' comes early. Why don't we go back up to the house now."

Her eyes slid to his, and he felt the impact straight through his gut to his spine. A few strands from her curls stuck to the dampness of her cheek.

"I'll be up in a bit."

Brody stared at her. She obviously didn't get the hint that he didn't want to leave her in the barn. Granted, he'd told her to make herself at home earlier, but this was stretching it just a little. More than a little. He didn't like her snooping about, no matter who her boss was. His first care was for his horses. He'd learned that a long time ago. And it had cost him.

"I insist. I insist you leave with me now. There will be time for you to look around tomorrow. With me."

He had nothing to hide, but he did have Prairie Rose to protect.

"Please… I just want some time to pull myself together."

"I'll just keep you company, then." He folded his arms.

She looked past his shoulder, out the door of the stall as if trying to figure out how to get away. Annoyed that she'd stopped giving her attention, Pretty dipped her head and nudged Lucy's hand.

"She likes you."

"I like her." Lucy pressed her face into the mane again. It was obvious she wasn't ready to leave yet, and he'd be damned if he'd leave her down here alone. Brody stepped a little to the side, leaning back against the fragrant wood of the box.

"Why?"

Lucy looked up. "Why what?"

"Why are you so interested in Pretty Piece? She's got years left, granted, but she's not what you came for."

Lucy rubbed her hand down the velvety nose. "No, she's not. She's a delightful surprise. I knew... I knew her mother."

To his chagrin her voice broke on the last word. Lord, not more tears.

"Let's get out of here," he demanded, stepping forward and gripping her arm. It was warm through the fleece she was wearing. "Before you upset the horses as well as yourself."

He led her out of the stall, and when she paused he tugged on her elbow.

"Stop." Her voice was sharp as she pulled out of his grasp.

"You want to talk about why you're crying, then? Because I want answers. Satisfying ones."

"I'm not crying for any specific reason." Her chin jutted out. "I just couldn't sleep."

He snorted something unintelligible.

She looked up at him then. "I *did* travel halfway across the world, you know."

Brody watched her keenly. This had nothing to do with jet lag, he knew it. And even though they'd argued earlier, he knew it wasn't about that, either. There was something else at the heart of it. What had she meant earlier when she'd muttered it wasn't fair?

He'd never been able to watch a woman cry, and he'd done his share in years past. That had been one of his biggest mistakes, and even knowing it he couldn't help the need to help that rose up in him. He wanted to believe her. To believe her motives were true even though her actions were suspect.

He took another step closer, close enough that if he extended his arm he'd be able to touch the tender skin of her bruised eyelids. Only inches away.

"What is it, Lucy? What is it about being here that upsets you so much?"

Lucy's fingers tightened, wrapping around each other in the absence of Pretty's coarse mane. She had to keep it together, because if she let go she'd realize exactly how close Brody was right now. The barn was so quiet she could hear the hum of the lights overhead. And still he watched her, waiting. Waiting for a reasonable explanation.

Brody was a deliberate man. She could tell that earlier. He did things a certain way and had definite opinions, and his initial one of her hadn't been favorable. And yet…he was waiting patiently for her. And she had no idea what to tell him. The truth was out of the question.

The sting of it was, when he looked at her this way, she wanted to tell him all manner of things, and she was sure he wouldn't understand.

No one understood.

Once again the feeling of total isolation. There was nothing familiar anymore, and the closest she'd gotten to it lately was here, tonight, surrounded by the scent of hay and horse and leather.

"Lucy?"

She couldn't help it. At the quiet verbalization of her name, the tears started afresh. Lucy. Who was that now? No one she knew.

"I hardly know you." It sounded pitiful to her ears but needed to be said.

He didn't answer, just absorbed everything through those black, damnably keen eyes of his. She was losing control and there was nothing she could do about it. But she would die rather than have him witness it.

"Please let me go," she tried, willing the words to come out strong and failing utterly. "I've embarrassed myself enough already. I shouldn't have come."

He stepped to one side.

She straightened her back, trying valiantly to gather what little bit of dignity she had left. Lucy blinked, sending teardrops over her lashes and down her cheeks as the homesickness overwhelmed her. She looked at the door. If she moved quickly she could get out and away from him. She'd been foolish to think she could belong here. She took one step, then another, her eyes blurring with tears.

And stumbled on a crack.

His arm was there to steady her in half a second, but her breath hitched in her chest and she sniffed. Brody turned her gently and pulled her into his arms.

The shock only lasted a millisecond. All the surprise of finding herself being held against him was swept away in the warm shelter of his arms, the rough feeling of his jean jacket against her cheek. She inhaled; the scent was somehow familiar. He was strong and steady and as his hand cradled her head, stroking her hair, she let go of all her grief in one sweeping wave.

He was a stranger. She was there on business. He'd questioned her and her integrity all in less than twenty-four hours. None of it mattered. He was a good man. He was *there*. That was what was important right now.

"Shhh." The sound rippled the hair above her ear, warming it with his breath. "It's okay."

Not in three long months had someone put their arms around her. No one had held her. No one had told her it would be okay.

Grief hit her, jolting the breath from her abdomen. She felt for a moment like she had the first time she'd been thrown and had hit the loam of the paddock. It had been a harder landing than she'd expected, and it had been difficult to get up.

Her arms slid around his waist, her fingers reaching up and biting into the denim covering his shoulder blades.

He tightened his grip around her, and one large hand massaged the back of her neck.

And all of the desolation Lucy had been holding inside came out in a grand rush of weeping, one that crashed on to the shore like a huge breaker and ebbed away on the tide, leaving her fragile, but feeling as though a burden had been taken from her shoulders.

She sniffed, sighed. And heard Brody's voice, rough and quiet.

"Lucy."

Her heart skipped around crazily. Not Miss Farnsworth, but Lucy. Tonight, in the intimacy of the barn, she'd become Lucy.

She stepped out of his arms. This was madness. She was tired and this was the middle of the night. He was a stranger. A very handsome one. It all jumbled together.

"I'm so sorry," she breathed, horrified at the splotches of moisture on his jean jacket. She couldn't meet his eyes. He already saw far too much. She didn't want him to see any more. She didn't want to see parts of him, either. There was a danger that she just might, and she took a step backward.

"Don't be."

"Forget this ever happened."

"Why don't you tell me what caused you to cry first?

Oh, where would she begin?

Pretty stamped behind them. Their presence there was disturbing the horses.

"There are actual chairs in the office," he said gently. "A kettle and a can of cookies. We can get to the bottom of this."

Lucy shook her head. "I've already made things uncomfortable. This won't happen again." She was pleased that her voice was coming out stronger with each word. She almost sounded convincing! "I'll just go back to the house."

But Brody persisted. "You're going to be staying here a while. You might as well tell me, because if you don't I'm going to wonder and you're going to hold it inside and it's just going to create friction. Hardly conducive to a profitable business trip."

He held out a hand. "Let me buy you an instant decaf."

She straightened her pullover. "Mr. Hamilton, I…"

But he interrupted. "You've just cried in my arms for a good ten minutes. You might

letting you in yet or not. A little bit of truth would go a long way."

Letting her in? That was the last thing she wanted.

"I'm here to do a job."

He crossed an ankle over his knee. "Yes, you are. And now I have more questions about you than answers, and that doesn't do much to inspire my trust."

"You, trust me? My fa— King Alexander's name should be enough." She tried to hide the near slip.

"Like I said earlier, I know enough about Navarro to know that His Highness only wants the best."

"Why do you need this alliance, anyway?" She jutted out her chin. What had seemed like a simple enough assignment on paper was rapidly getting complicated. She hadn't counted on a stubborn rancher who didn't know how to mind his own business!

"Are you kidding? Everyone knows about Navarro stables. An alliance with the royal family of Marazur could change everything."

She pursed her lips, putting her cup down on the desk and folding her arms. "You clearly will gain more than we will, then. It's not in your best interest to question."

Brody raised an eyebrow. "And if you went back empty-handed?"

Her scowl faded. That was out of the question. This was all she had left. She had to prove herself to her father. And that meant proving herself to Brody now.

Brody persisted. "He's sent you to me. Face it. We need each other."

"What do you want from me?" She hid her face behind the rim of her mug. She was still feeling too raw, and their verbal sparring had only been a placebo against the pain; the reason why she'd sneaked down here in the middle of the night in the first place. She'd wanted to be away from prying eyes. To be somewhere that she felt even a little bit at home. She had wanted to have her cry—the one that had been building all day—in private. Get it over with, with no one the wiser. Now she was having to deal with that *and* an angry Brody.

"I want to know why you were in my barn in the middle of the night, crying."

"It's private."

With an impatient huff, Brody stood and put his cup down on the desk. "Have it your way," he said shortly, turning to the door.

Had she honestly thought he'd accept that answer? She supposed it would have been too much to ask for some understanding. Maybe he'd used up his quota holding her outside Pretty's stall. But she could tell by the set of his jaw that the next days were going to be very difficult if they were working from different sides.

Her mouth opened and closed several times but no words would come out. Instead the only sound was Brody's boots on the cement floor.

She couldn't let him leave. If he refused to negotiate, she'd go back to Marazur a failure and that was the one thing she *couldn't* do.

"Brody, wait!"

She ran to the door and braced her hands on the frame. "Wait."

He stopped. Turned back around.

And her heart did that skip thing again.

It was supposed to be easy. An escape. Not a sexy cowboy who felt a need to pry into her personal business and was using her professional needs as blackmail.

"If you must know, I grew up in Virginia. Around horses. My mum…she was a bookkeeper for a farm there. That's how I knew

Pretty's dam, Pretty Colleen. She was at Trembling Oak when I was a child, before she was sold. This place…it reminds me of there."

"You're homesick?" He didn't sound as if he quite believed her. His voice echoed hollowly through the barn.

"Yes…but there's more. My mum…" She paused, swallowing against the sudden lump that lodged in her throat. "My mum died a few months ago. There've been so many changes…" Her words drifted into ether. She blinked once, twice. Inhaled, gathering strength. "So many changes lately that I haven't had time to grieve. Being here today seemed to set me off, that's all. And I needed to be with…with someone who understood."

"Pretty," he replied, an indulgent smile in his voice.

"Don't make fun of me." Her eyes flashed at him. Was it so hard to understand that she'd found a link to her home in the horse, in Prairie Rose? Surely he wasn't that blind.

He came closer. "I'm not making fun." He stopped, the toes of his boots mere inches from her sneakers. "It's the first thing you've said that made perfect sense."

She lifted her gaze and met his. With the

animosity and grief suddenly drained away, there was nothing standing between them, and Lucy felt the unadulterated pull of attraction.

"Was that so hard?" His question was a soft murmur.

"Yes," she whispered back.

"I know," he replied, those two words evoking so many questions she now wanted to ask.

He cupped her jaw, ran a rough thumb over her cheekbone. "Thank you for telling me. It explains a lot."

She swallowed, tried to inhale, but the air seemed thin. Another inch and he would be in kissing distance. She shouldn't be thinking about kissing him....

"Let's go back up now. Tomorrow's a long day."

Lucy stepped back, offered what she hoped passed for a smile and followed him out of the barn.

She'd said more than she'd planned...how could she have mentioned Trembling Oak? And she'd been talking to the horse when he'd burst into the box. Had he overheard any of what she'd said?

He already knew too much. She'd have to be much more careful. No more midnight revelations. From now on it had to be strictly business!

Chapter Four

Brody looked up from his breakfast when he heard her steps on the stairs.

And then looked down again, spearing another chunk of scrambled egg on his fork and ignoring the queer lifting in his chest. He wasn't looking forward to seeing her. He couldn't be. That was just plain ridiculous.

He'd been crazy last night. Finding her in Pretty's stall had raised all sorts of alarm bells, but by the end of it...

He scowled. He'd been a fool. A soft touch. He should know better by now. Instead he'd listened to her story and he'd...hell, he'd even *touched* her at the end. His fork dropped to his plate. Touched her soft, white skin with its faint smattering of freckles.

And he'd thought about kissing her.

Yup. A fool. A fool to forget who she was, where she was from. A fool to be distracted by the sight of tears on her lashes, and a fool for wanting somehow to make it better. He picked up his fork again and defiantly shoved another piece of egg into his mouth. Oh, no. He'd fallen into that trap before.

"Good morning."

He looked up, schooling his features into what he hoped was a general expression of disinterest. "Good morning."

Her cheeks were pink and her lips were slightly puffy, as though she'd been chewing on them. "Breakfast was fifteen minutes ago." He couldn't resist adding the shot.

He was gratified to see her blush a little before he looked back down at his plate.

"I'm sorry. I... I overslept."

Yeah. As if he didn't know why. He stretched out his legs, glad that he wasn't the only one who was running on short sleep. He raised an eyebrow in her direction.

"I didn't sleep that well."

"I'm sorry to hear that." And then felt about two inches tall as he saw the confused, wounded look on her face. He was being a jerk and he knew it.

"It doesn't matter, Lucy." Mrs. Polcyk came from the kitchen with a plate in her hands and a smile on her face. "You just sit right up now. Brody's out of sorts this morning."

He scowled. There were disadvantages to having a housekeeper that had known him since he'd been a boy in boots too big for his feet. First Martha yesterday and now Mrs. P. Yet he knew the women around here well enough to know they always considered the men their "boys," thinking that living with them excused lots of things. He looked up at Mrs. P. who merely angled an eyebrow at him. They'd been through hell together, and he had to admit it did excuse a lot. He wouldn't dress her down for the world. He gritted his teeth but said nothing. He knew he was reacting unreasonably. But he'd be damned if he'd give an apology. It was probably better to keep Lucy at arm's length anyway. He looked away and grabbed the carafe of coffee from the table, refilling his cup.

Lucy spread jam on her toast and looked up at him. "I thought this morning maybe I could have a look at your files."

She was speaking directly to him and he

was obligated to look at her. He did, noticing how her tongue ran out over her lip even though she tried to make her eyes look brave. So she was nervous. Good. She'd taken enough liberties last night. He folded his hands in front of him and faced her squarely.

"I've got things to do."

"If you'll just point the way…"

Brody's eyebrows snapped together. "Point the way? And leave you alone?"

"What do you think I'm going to do, Brody?" Her toast dropped back to her plate and she stopped worrying her lips. They were plump and prettily pink. Like they'd been last night in the barn.

What did he think? He ignored his fascination with her lips and leaned back in his chair. What he thought was that those who trusted too easily got burned, and that his trust had to be earned, not expected. He'd spent enough time doing damage control because someone got a little bit nosy with the particulars of Prairie Rose Ranch. He wouldn't let that happen again.

"Who knows? After last night…"

Mrs. P. banged a pan in the pantry, and both Brody and Lucy fell momentarily silent. He looked at her across the table. The truth was he'd been able to understand her actions last night more than she knew. How many times had he taken solace in the barns when things got to be too much? He understood the need for connection. The need to grieve and not feeling able to.

But this was a new day. It was not shadows in a quiet barn, instant coffee and confessions. There could not be anything personal between them. The last thing he wanted was for her to delve too deeply, and the thought of her riffling through his records and files made him set his jaw. He'd hoped she wasn't one of those people who put more stock in paper trails than in horseflesh. He didn't put much credence in that, and he was a long way from trusting her.

He looked away from her steady eyes and instead added pepper to his already sufficiently peppered eggs. The truth was, he didn't know exactly what she planned to do with whatever information she found. There was more to Lucy than a simple emissary. He just didn't know *what*. That was the problem. He doubted it was just about breeding records. Yet what more could she want?

"I thought you might like to go for a ride this morning. See more of the ranch."

Lucy forced herself not to sigh. She'd thought she'd made some headway last night in getting Brody to trust her, but he was clearly putting her off this morning. The half-hearted invitation to go for a ride was simply to offer a diversion. She knew he didn't want to be near her any more than she really wanted to be near him. He just didn't want her snooping around. What was he hiding?

She wanted to ask him, but she knew he wouldn't answer. And right now she had to bite her tongue and try to keep things civil.

It was completely reasonable for her to want to look at his breeding history. She had to make the right decisions for Navarro if she was going to prove herself. She wanted to see bloodlines, combinations, strengths and weaknesses before she signed on the dotted line. He should know this. He should trust her to do her job.

Which meant he had another reason for putting her off. She didn't like the thought of that very much.

She sliced through a piece of fried ham. "And I'd like to do that, but another time. I'd like to get an overall picture of your program here first." She wanted dates, names, records. To see his strengths and weaknesses and think about how they could benefit Navarro. And even…how Navarro could benefit him.

"And if I refuse?" He raised an eyebrow.

"Then I'm wasting my time." Heart in her throat, she pushed back her chair and started to put her napkin beside her plate.

"Fine."

She stopped, half up and half down. Relief rushed through her; he wasn't calling her bluff.

"Finish your breakfast, princess. When you're done I'll dig out the files you need."

For the tiniest second she froze, immobilized by the idea that he'd somehow clued in to who she was. Struggling to compose herself, she sat back in her chair and silently steamed. Nothing she had said could have revealed her true identity to him. Which meant…which meant he was using it as a nickname. And she didn't like the snarky twist he added to it, either. It certainly wasn't meant as a compliment.

She met his gaze coldly. "Thank you."

Wordlessly Brody got up, gathered his plate and coffee cup and took them to the kitchen before stalking out.

Lucy sat for a moment, thinking she should

feel as if she'd won a victory, but somehow didn't. Brody wouldn't know why she felt she had to succeed here, or why she needed to prove herself.

He was making it difficult right from the get-go. He intimidated her and she hated that. It made every rebellious fiber in her rise up and want to be counted, a trait that had got her into trouble too many times as a child. Which didn't necessarily help in the "get what you want" scheme of things. She drained her coffee cup and put it down. Yet… it wasn't in her to simper and play at pretending. She wasn't good at it.

Which is what made this whole farce even more difficult.

She turned the cup over in her hands, running her thumb over the Prairie Rose insignia on its side. She'd come downstairs wondering if they were going to be awkward with each other and had been met with annoying belligerence.

Perhaps that was good, because he wouldn't ask personal questions. But this trip was rapidly feeling as if she was beating her head against a wall and making little progress. She put the mug down.

Why had he been so angry this morning?

Last night he'd ended up being kind...even gentle. For a moment she'd thought he was going to kiss her.

Mrs. Polcyk stopped by her shoulder and refilled her coffee cup.

"Mrs. Polcyk, did I do something wrong this morning?" The housekeeper reminded her of Mrs. Pendleton, the wife of the owner of Trembling Oak. Mrs. Pendleton had never given herself airs; she'd baked pecan pie and cooked grits and had always made time for talks with Lucy in her kitchen. It was easier for Lucy to ask it of the motherly housekeeper than Brody. Mrs. Polcyk patted her shoulder, and Lucy almost thought she heard a sigh.

"Brody's a private man, Lucy. That's all."

"But...but I'm here to *help* his business. I don't understand why he made such a point of not wanting me to have a look at the breeding records. I need to see where Ahab's progeny have gone and how they've performed." She stopped short of mentioning the previous night in the barn.

Mrs. Polcyk went to the cupboard and took out another mug, poured herself a cup of coffee and took the seat Brody had vacated.

"I think you're a good girl, Lucy, and I'm

not the suspicious type like Brody is. But he's got good reason to be careful."

She took a drink of her coffee and looked down the hall toward the study.

"You're not going to explain that further, are you."

The housekeeper smiled thinly. Lucy thought she saw a hint of sadness in the grayish blue eyes. "In this case I don't think it's my story to tell. What I *can* tell you is that Brody has put his heart and soul into making Prairie Rose what it is today. It's everything to him."

"I can understand that."

"I know you can." She reached over and patted Lucy's hand. "For what it's worth, he wants this deal to work. He needs to up our profile, and an alliance with you will do that."

"Then why does he keep fighting me? I've been here less than twenty-four hours and I already know if I say black, he'll say white."

Mrs. Polcyk got up from the table, taking both their cups. "Because the only thing more important than an alliance with King Alexander is protecting what he loves. If he thinks that in some way you'll threaten Prairie Rose, the choice will be easy for him. He's put his heart and soul into this place." Mrs. Polcyk

paused and gazed out the window for a moment, and Lucy could have sworn she saw
the older woman's lips tremble a little as she
murmured, "Perhaps too much."

She cleared her throat and nodded at Lucy.
"You go on to the office now, just down the
hall at the end. Brody'll have everything set
out for you, despite his earlier attitude."

Lucy smoothed her hair and ran her hands
over her T-shirt, down the thighs of her jeans.

Mrs. Polcyk meant well, but now Lucy
had more questions than answers. What had
Brody sacrificed for the ranch? What had
been threatened before? What was it that
made him build a wall around himself whenever she was around?

She looked down the hall at the closed
door. Perhaps a morning spent with breeding
records would tell her more than she could
get out of either the housekeeper *or* Brody.

Lucy rubbed her eyes; they were drying
out in the hot prairie air. She'd been most of
the day going over Brody's files, and the only
thing she felt was impressed.

Over the past several years, he'd taken Prairie Rose Ranch and moved it from strength to
strength as far as she could tell. His decisions

made sense, for the most part. She liked how he kept his own quarter horse stock fairly undiluted and with solid bloodlines. It was a grassroots approach that clearly worked for him and he knew it. She could see it in his decisions right here on paper.

And she could see it in what she'd seen of his horses. She'd caught a glimpse of a stallion last night that had been breathtaking. She could already envision the offspring from him and their newly acquired Thoroughbred mare. Her father—King Alexander—had emphasized his desire to breed quarter horses with his Thoroughbreds, and she agreed with him completely. Each had qualities that, when combined, would make wonderful polo ponies. King Alexander was looking for those traits of speed and agility.

She closed the last file folder and checked her watch. Nearly six. Where had the time gone? She noted the mess of notes she'd taken on the desk and knew she should tidy it up, leave the office as neatly as she'd found it. She tamped the papers together and lined everything up on the blotter. If she just had a paperclip to keep her notes straight.

She slid open the first drawer, but it had nothing in it but a brick of pristine paper, presumably for the printer. She slid it closed and opened the next one. Bingo. Pens, a stapler, a pair of scissors.

She was putting everything back in order when she realized she'd missed a file. It was inside one of the others, and she tapped her bottom lip as she opened it and scanned the records within. Everything Brody had given her this morning had gone back about six years, maybe a little more. But this file was older...closer to eight years. She saw the signature on page after page—not Brody's but John Hamilton's. Then there were a few pages with Brody's scrawl across the bottom. Her brow wrinkled as she rechecked the date. There was a gap of nearly a year— nearly a year of records missing. She knew it was impossible that he hadn't bought or sold any horses in that time, or hadn't participated in any breeding whatsoever. It was almost as if...

Lucy chewed her bottom lip. Almost as if the ranch had ceased to exist for a solid year. She wondered what story the bank records would tell, but she had no access to them, nor did she imagine Brody would give them to her.

A door slammed, and Lucy quickly shut

the file, putting it back at the bottom of the pile. She was just putting the clip over her sheaf of papers when Brody stepped into the office.

He spared her a look, raised his eyebrows slightly and asked, "Did you find what you were looking for?"

She wondered, not for the first time, what had happened to put that distrustful chip on his shoulder. Did it have something to do with the lapse she'd found in his filing system? She itched to ask him, but looking at his scowling face, she knew this wasn't the time. "I did. And then some," she couldn't help adding.

His eyes narrowed a little, and she couldn't help but laugh. The imp in her—the part she'd been hiding for so long—wanted out to play. The best thing would be for him to offer the information voluntarily, and there was no way that would happen if they kept snapping at each other. "The only thing I didn't find in your files is evidence of your shoe size."

She'd wanted him to laugh, to lighten up. But at his continued quizzical glare, her own smile faded.

"I'm not going to win with you, am I." It was a statement rather than a question. She gathered up her sheets and came around to the front of the desk. He stepped aside but not far enough. When she went to go through the door, his body was too close to hers and she quivered with sudden awareness. It was as if she was back to the night before, in the dark intimacy of the barn. His size didn't intimidate her; perhaps it would be easier if it did. But in the moment that she paused at the door, she felt the strength in him and wondered what kind of woman could possibly resist his sort of sexy stability.

"Problem, princess?"

She swallowed, feeling the blush flood her cheeks at his dark, knowing words. They were meant as a taunt, but he couldn't know how they added fuel to the fire already flickering within her. "Uh, no," she murmured, and headed out the door and away.

"Dinner's on in five minutes," he called after her as she fled to the stairs. She took them two at a time and hurried to her room, closing the door and leaning against it.

First last night, and now in the study. This was not in the plan at all.

Because she was curious about Brody Hamilton. And not all of it had to do with Prairie Rose or Navarro. A good healthy portion of it was a woman responding to a man.

Desire. And she had no idea how to deal with it and still do her job.

When she went downstairs, she could smell dinner rather than see it. She followed the delectable scent to the deck and found Brody flipping steaks with a set of metal tongs. She moved past him to lean against the railing of the small deck. It faced south; she looked slightly to the right and could just pick out the hazy ridge of the mountains. It was so flat here. A person could see for miles and miles.

And feel very small and insignificant. She should be used to that feeling by now. Lord knew she felt that way most of the time in Marazur.

"Is there anything I can do to help?" She pasted on a polite smile and hoped she didn't blush again. Brody'd put his hat back on out in the afternoon sun and it shaded his face too much. She couldn't see his expression.

Mrs. Polcyk bustled through the door, carrying a tray of dishes and cutlery. "Let me take that," Lucy insisted, jumping to help, and hiding from Brody's gaze behind the weight of the tray. "I feel silly doing nothing."

"How do you like your steak?"

She paused from putting out cutlery and

looked up. Lord, he was ornery, and his reticence was driving her insane, but she couldn't deny his good looks or his physical presence, or her reaction to them. Even scowling, he was impressive. "Medium," she answered.

He nodded beneath his black hat, and she wished he'd take it off again so she could see his eyes. And she wished they would stop arguing all the time. Her pride dictated she go toe-to-toe with him. But the lonely girl in her wanted to see him as an ally, a friend. She'd been going it alone for some time now. She wasn't sure she could keep it up much longer without turning bitter. She finished laying out the plates and went to him.

"Brody." She laid her hand on his arm, surprised to feel the muscle tense beneath her fingers. She stared at the spot where their skin met for a fleeting second, the warmth shooting through her veins. She swallowed. Forced herself to look him in the eye beneath the brim of his hat. She'd been seeing this all from her point of view. What if she were in Brody's shoes? She'd never considered herself selfish before, but her thoughts over the past few months changed her mind. She'd spent so much time resenting what her life had become that she'd forgotten to put herself in other people's shoes. She had so many questions she wished she could ask him: about the family he didn't seem to have, about the ranch. But she got the feeling he was hiding hurts, and she needed to remember she wasn't the only one who'd been dealt a cruel hand. She needed to apologize to him and perhaps start them over on a new footing.

"I didn't mean to make things tense this morning. I… I only wanted to see your records so that when I see the rest of your operation I can put it in context. I want to make the best decision for Navarro and that means learning as much as possible. I hope you understand that's where I was coming from. It wasn't meant to be…oh, I don't know what I'm trying to say. I just want you to know I'm not out to hurt Prairie Rose." *Or you,* she thought, but held the words inside.

Once the words were out, her breath caught for a second before she inhaled again. His eyes, those lovely dark onyx eyes, slid over her face. The meat sizzled on the grill beside them and a kingbird called from a nearby shrub, but for a few suspended seconds their gazes caught, held, while her hand remained on his arm. During those seconds Lucy had the same crazy sensation she'd had last night when she'd thought about kissing him.

Her tongue ran over her lip. Kissing big Brody Hamilton.

Now that would be a learning experience.

Her breath shuddered inward, and Brody took a step back and away from her touch.

"Yes, well, in my opinion you don't learn about an operation by trusting what you see on paper. You've got a long way to go to inspire my trust, Miss Farnsworth."

Last night she'd been Lucy. Now it was back to Miss Farnsworth, just as in the study.

It was probably for the best.

"Do you trust my... King Alexander?"

"I don't know."

She stepped back, unsure of how to proceed. Mrs. Polcyk returned and put a couple of salad bowls on the table, seemingly oblivious to the tension shimmering around them.

"Those steaks about ready, Brody?"

He spared Mrs. P. a glance, then looked back down at the grill. "Not quite."

Lucy turned toward the housekeeper. "Is there anything I can do, Mrs. P.?"

Brody's head snapped around so quickly she wondered that he didn't give himself whiplash.

"Not a thing, dear. Once the steaks are done, we'll have a nice dinner." She looked at Brody who was scowling darkly. "Though Brody's beer's almost gone. You could get him another, and one for me, too, if you don't mind. This heat…"

Lucy escaped to the coolness of the kitchen. She could hear Brody's voice and Mrs. P.'s sharp reply through the window, but not what they were saying. When she returned to the deck with three bottles, Mrs. P. was settled in a chair with a satisfied air, and Brody smiled stiffly as she twisted off the cap and handed him the beer.

"Thanks."

It was polite, but she could tell he didn't really mean it.

Lucy sat at the table across from Mrs. Polcyk, wondering how this could possibly be any more awkward. She'd apologized and he'd basically handed it back to her. Politely, but handed it back just the same. The only thing that would make it worse would be if he knew who she really was, she thought with a grimace. At least now she could kick back with a beer and enjoy a steak.

"One medium." Brody placed the steak on her plate and moved on to Mrs. P. The smell was tantalizing. At Mrs. P.'s urging, she added potato salad and tossed salad to her plate.

For a few moments no one said anything. Lucy wondered if the sounds of chewing were going to take the place of polite meal-time conversation. She wished it had when Mrs. Polcyk decided that the time should be spent finding out more about *her*.

"How do you know King Alexander, Lucy?"

The potato salad got thick in her mouth, and she chewed, tried to swallow. Suddenly her earlier explanation to Brody wasn't enough. And briefly she considered telling him exactly what her relationship was to His Highness. But he already didn't trust her, and he would trust her even less if he knew she was on a daughter's errand. He didn't believe she knew what she was doing. And telling him she was the king's daughter would wipe away any hope of credibility.

She paused so long that Brody put down his fork and knife. He'd removed his hat before sitting down to eat, and there was no evading his piercing eyes this time.

"Yes, Lucy, exactly how *do* you know the king?"

Mrs. P. angled him a sharp look at his caustic tone, but Lucy knew she was well and truly caught. Her mind worked feverishly, trying to find a way to tell the truth without *really* telling the truth.

"He knew my mother," she managed, trying to make her voice casual and demonstrating her outward relaxation by spearing a piece of cucumber and popping it in her mouth. If only they knew how uncomfortable she was on the inside, perhaps they'd stop asking questions!

Then she looked at Brody and realized her discomfort was probably a fringe benefit to him. She chewed with gusto and pasted on a smile. If ever she needed acting ability, now was the time.

"King Alexander has always dabbled in the horse business," she explained as breezily as she could muster. "I mentioned that I grew up in Virginia—" she looked at Brody for confirmation "—and my mum ran the office for Trembling Oak. She'd met Alexander—still a crown prince at the time—when he was on one of his extended trips.

"I spent years working in the stables. When the time came that my mum was ill, she thought perhaps I'd like to travel, see the world. Thought perhaps King Alexander would hire me in Marazur. I could travel and work at what I loved at the same time."

"Which he obviously did. But why would he do it? He didn't really know you, did he?"

"No, I'd never met him before."

Suddenly she couldn't push down the lump that formed in her throat. Both Brody's and Mrs. P.'s eyes were on her, and she forced a bright smile. "Why does anyone do anything? The main thing is he *did* decide to hire me and so far he hasn't regretted it. I'm good at what I do. I have a good eye."

There, she'd done it. She'd laid out the history without Brody being the wiser. Anyone who saw her would never put two and two together. She looked nothing like her father. He had the Navarro dark, Mediterranean looks, and she had her mother's curly burnished hair and pale skin.

Brody pushed back his plate. "Great salad, Mrs. P. But then, it always is."

"Aren't you staying for dessert?"

He shook his head, pushing back his chair and standing. He grabbed his hat from the knob on the end of the deck post. "No, thanks. I have some things to do. I'll grab some later when I come in."

"Do you want some help?" Lucy looked

up. She'd really hoped that her partial story would be taken as an olive branch. After all, she knew next to nothing about Brody, and already he knew more about her than she'd wanted to tell. But he shook his head.

"No, you enjoy your evening." He paused. "You've got free rein in the office tomorrow. I have some business to take care of away from the ranch."

He spun on his heel without a further good-bye and hopped off the deck, leaving Lucy gaping at his snappish exit while Mrs. Polcyk calmly ate her potato salad.

Chapter Five

She'd had enough of looking at paperwork.

Lucy closed the cabinet and pushed back in the rolling chair, the casters settling in comfortable grooves in the plastic mat beneath the desk. There was only so much to learn from paper, and even after searching today, she still didn't have any answers as to what happened to the missing year. And she'd been inside long enough. She knew Brody didn't want her snooping around—not after the other night in the barn. He seemed quite territorial that way. But it was a gorgeous day, and she had a need to be outside in the fresh air with the birds and the scent of grass and the horses.

She pulled on her boots at the door. Maybe she'd pay a visit to Pretty and take her an apple. The poor girl had been cooped up just as she had—inside on a beautiful summer's day.

The sky was a heartbreaking blue and the air hot and dry as Lucy wended her way through the yard to the barn. She filled her lungs, absorbing the smell of sweetgrass from the surrounding fields. She didn't mind the isolation here. It was welcoming. She thought briefly about her new home in Marazur. More people around, more activity. Servants and business, parties and meetings. All things so foreign to her that it was no wonder she hid in the stables most of the time. She definitely felt more lonely there than here. Even with Brody's surliness, Prairie Rose was far more familiar to her than the high-class Navarro stables. Loneliness wasn't about people, she realized. It was about being comfortable with your place in the world. Now she lived in a palace where the occupants were distant strangers. Trembling Oak had been her place. Prairie Rose was the closest she'd been to that in a long time.

Pretty's box was empty when she arrived, and she wondered if the farrier had come back to check on the hoof. The barn was quiet; in the middle of summer most of the stock was outside. She smiled, trailing her hand along a smooth railing. Why wouldn't they be? That would have been her choice, too.

As she got close to the middle of the barn she heard voices coming from the riding ring.

She left the railing behind and made her way to the double doors leading to the enclosed ring. It was cool inside, and her feet sunk a bit in the soft loam. For a moment she paused and smiled. It reminded her so much of her childhood days, training for her pleasure classes. Putting her horse through the paces after school, then heading back to the kitchen for a snack on the sly.

A couple of hands were standing in the center of the ring, with Pretty attached to a long lead. And that's when Lucy's smile faded.

"She looks good, Bill. Might as well call Martha and save her a trip. No harm in lettin' her out for a bit now."

Lucy approached, her eyes on Pretty even as the words registered. Martha was the far-

rier. It had only been a few days since Pretty
had picked up the bruise. Did Brody know
what these men were about to do?

The mare should definitely be seen before being set loose. At the very least, Brody
should be the one to pronounce her fit. It was
what she'd do if it were her operation.

She set her lips. Something wasn't quite
right.

"Lengthen your lead and take her up and
back," she commanded from across the ring.

The two men turned to her, eyebrows
raised as she strode forward.

"Beg your pardon?"

"You heard me. Give her more lead, take
her up and bring her back."

The one she assumed was Bill touched his
cap but his eyes were cold. "And you are?"

She paused only feet away. "Lucy Farnsworth."

He smiled politely but she knew she wasn't
getting far. Her name meant nothing to them.

"Well, Miss Farnsworth, unless we hear
from Mr. Hamilton…"

"You'll what? Forgo a visit from the farrier and then be responsible for a lame horse?
A prize-winning mare? Be my guest. But I
wouldn't want to be on the receiving end of

Mr. Hamilton's anger when he realizes you've crippled her because you were lazy and taking shortcuts."

She stopped and shoved her hands in her pockets.

The man met her eyes steadily. She knew she was right and she could see the mention of Brody had him doubting his wisdom.

"I guess I can humor you. Though you'll just see she's doing fine." He looked over his shoulder at his companion. "Give her more lead and trot her out."

Lucy stepped forward, watching closely as Pretty moved away from her. When she came back she noticed it, but she had to be sure.

"A couple of turns, please."

Wordlessly they took Pretty in a half circle, turned and came the other direction. Yes, there it was. She had no doubt now.

"That mare is still lame."

"I didn't see nothin'."

"Then you're blind. Look how she lifts her head. It's not big, but it's there."

She strode over to Pretty, gave her a pat and rubbed her nose. "Hey, girl. What's up?"

She looked over at the men. "One of you going to help me or what?"

The man named Bill came over, scowling.

"Mr. Hamilton doesn't like outsiders messing with his stock," he growled.

"And how does he feel about incompetence?" she asked coolly. "Here, hold her a moment."

With Bill's hand on the mare's halter, Lucy bent and ran her hands down the foreleg. No tenderness here, but…she paused. There was heat, on the hoof. She nudged and Pretty obliged by lifting her foot, and Lucy did a brief inspection. There didn't seem to be any cuts, but that didn't mean she couldn't have been pricked and it had been missed. Infection? Hard to know. She stood, moved over to the other side and went through the same procedure.

"What's going on here?"

Brody's voice rang through the ring and Lucy jumped, went back and started over. She could hear his boots approaching but focused on her job at the moment. No, she'd been right. There was definitely heat on the other hoof wall and slight swelling on one side only. This side was cooler.

"Bill. What's going on?"

His voice was hard and Lucy shored her shoulders for the blast she knew was coming and for the courage she'd need to face it.

"She came in and started giving orders. I told her you wouldn't like it."

Lucy stood, wiping her hands on her jeans. "Hey, Brody." She made her voice deliberately casual but it failed miserably. His scowl was more pronounced than ever.

"I thought you were in with the paperwork."

"I was. I finished. I went for a walk and ended up here. Good thing, too."

"Is that right."

He was outright scornful and her temper flared. "That's right. Your men were going to give Pretty Piece here a clean bill of health. And that would have been a huge mistake."

"Says you." He snorted, starting to turn away.

"Says you, if you listen for two minutes!" she shouted.

Bill and his companion backed away slowly.

Brody turned back and treated her to a look of pure bored indulgence. "Look, Bill and Arnie have been with Prairie Rose for years. I trust their judgment."

"So you won't even listen to what I have to say? You arrogant jerk! You'll risk a lame mare because you're too proud to what? Take advice from a whippersnapper like me?"

His lips quivered. "Whippersnapper?"

"Shut up." The words she was thinking of were much more pithy but she didn't utter them.

The men's mouths had dropped open at the word *jerk* and had yet to close, but she ignored them and the heat that flushed her cheeks at knowing she'd lost her cool. His obvious humor at her choice of words bugged her, too, but she pushed it aside, trying to make her point.

"You think that I don't know what I'm doing because why? Because I'm young? Because I'm a woman? You decided the moment I got here who I was and you put me in a convenient little box."

For the moment he looked so nonplussed he didn't speak. Well bully for him.

"You judged me and decided I didn't have anything valuable to add. You would have sent me on my merry way if King Alexander hadn't been involved. And you know what that makes you?" Her eyes flashed as his darkened and a muscle ticked in his jaw. "One of the good old boys. A chauvinist. I've seen lots of them in this business. It didn't stop me then and it won't stop me now. I'm good at what I do. I'm really good! I've earned my place and I know it even if no one else does!"

She broke off abruptly, her heart pounding and the backs of her eyes pricking painfully. That felt good. For months it had been about being Mary Ellen's daughter, or Princess Luciana. As if who she was inside didn't really matter. As if all the work she'd put in over the years meant nothing compared to a promise.

"Are you done?"

She nodded. "For the moment."

He stepped forward. Bill and Arnie were long gone; once she'd started her diatribe they'd fled. Her heart fluttered as he stepped through the soft loam of the ring until he was close enough she had to look up to see his face.

"My trust needs to be earned. And I don't trust easily and certainly not with my livelihood. Your affiliation with the king is all that's kept you here, you do realize that."

She swallowed. She'd been right on that score, then. It infuriated her. She hadn't even met King Alexander until a few months ago!

"You weren't what I expected, that's true. I *was* surprised that Navarro had sent a very young, very pretty girl to negotiate an important deal. That was flag number one. Then you came and I caught you snooping the first night. That was flag number two. And then you were determined to spend time with my files. I've seen people like you. Ones who are more concerned with bottom lines and what things look like on paper rather than reality." His arm swept wide. "*This* is reality. And it's the *last* place you've come, rather than the first."

She took a breath and exhaled slowly, knowing another outburst wouldn't help her case and she was still reeling from the fact that he'd called her young and pretty. She pushed her female vanity aside; it was as irrelevant as her age or her gender. "Just because I took a different approach than you would doesn't make it wrong. And it doesn't mean I don't know what I'm doing. If you take the word of those men over mine, it'll make for larger problems later. You want a chance to trust me? This is it."

"All right then. What makes you think they are wrong?"

"I had them trot her out. It's not that obvious, but it's there if you look. I think she's developed an infection. The hoof wall is hot and she's showing signs."

He regarded her carefully. She still had her hand on Pretty's halter and she met his gaze fully. She could tell he was curious but not entirely convinced. This was her chance to prove to him she knew her stuff. "Don't take my word for it. Let me show you."

Lucy paced off a few steps and trotted out the mare, pointing out the tiny bob of the head each time she stepped on the affected hoof. Bringing her back, she showed Brody the hoof. "It doesn't look like anything, but the wall's warm. Warmer than the other. I used the same hand to be sure. I'm not imagining it, Brody."

Brody put the hoof down and straightened, rubbing Pretty's withers and frowning.

"No you're not. You're right."

"Thank you."

"I suppose you expect an apology now for what I said."

She smiled wryly. "You don't strike me as the apologetic type." She lifted her chin. "You meant every word you said. So did I."

His eyes warmed. "Then I won't say I'm sorry if you won't."

"That's fine, then."

"How about if I just concede that you are right about the mare and that you seem to be more knowledgeable than I originally thought."

Her lips curved slightly. "That'll do."

He took one more step. Her breath caught at his nearness and he lifted his hand. She wondered if he was going to touch her. She wanted him to touch her. Even after the words they'd hurled at each other, she still wanted it.

But his hand moved past her shoulder and gripped Pretty's halter. Lucy took her hand off the nylon.

"So in your opinion, what she needs is…"

He waited for her to answer. He was giving her a chance to show she could make the right call.

"Antibiotics and anti-inflammatories. Probably a five-day course of each. If that doesn't clear it up, then call the vet. But I really think that will do it."

"I agree."

She had to go now. It had been difficult to argue with him but it was more difficult to stand there and act unaffected. The trouble was, she'd meant all she'd said. And she still found herself drawn to him. To his strength and conviction. How could that be?

She nodded and started to walk away.

"Lucy."

She turned back. He had his hand on the halter but was facing her. "Thank you."

It would have to do. From Brody there wouldn't be praise and acknowledgment of her expertise. She'd been correct and he'd said thank you. It was all she'd get and she knew it. But she wanted more. She'd come here to do a job and here in the ring it had been about Pretty and about proving something to him. She'd done that. And now she found she wanted approval, not just of her skills but for herself.

Brody was starting to matter. And he couldn't, not when she had to leave so very soon. She couldn't let his opinion of her matter. It would only hurt in the end, and life had hurt her enough lately.

"You're welcome," she replied, but spun on her heel and kept walking until she was back outside in the heat again.

"I've saddled the gelding for you."

Lucy stared down the corridor at Brody. For several days they'd crossed paths as she learned more about the ranch, and he'd been slightly warmer, with perhaps a hint of grudging respect. Last night he'd been quiet at dinner but at the end had suggested they go for a ride around Prairie Rose so she could see more of the outlying areas of the ranch. He hadn't said as much, but she had supposed it was his way of showing his approval of her. Of admitting in a roundabout way that she knew what she was doing. Only now she wasn't sure at all, because he'd picked a past-his-prime gelding for her to ride out on.

"Seriously?" She'd had her eye on the bay, the large magnificent one she'd seen the other night. Brody led the gelding out, a gray Appaloosa with a blanket of gorgeous spots on his hindquarters. A beautiful boy just the same, but she could tell he was slowing down. He'd be tame. Too tame for her. She wanted to feel the wind in her hair and the power beneath her. She gritted her teeth. She thought they'd cleared the air yesterday, but his choice of mount for her was patronizing. Clearly her job wasn't done if he thought the gelding was the best she could handle.

"If you think I can't handle a more spirited mount, think again."

Brody smiled slowly. "You know, I get the feeling life is never boring with you, Lucy. You have this need to challenge *everything*."

"And you think that's funny?" She planted her hands on her hips. His grin was a surprise, a teasing, lopsided smile that was hard to resist. He ran hot and cold, she realized, and wondered why that was. Since that day in the corral, he'd been cool and remote, almost angry at her picking up on Pretty's injury. Even at the end when he'd admitted she was right, praise had been sparse and certainly not teasing. Today he seemed to have shed all that animosity and at least seemed equitable. What had changed between last night and this morning? "You're very lucky I challenged your men."

His smile faded into seriousness. "I know that. You picked up on what they missed. I'm grateful."

"But you still don't trust me with your prized horses?" She raised her eyebrows at the gelding. "You don't think I can handle them?"

"That's not it at all!" He scowled. "Lord, you try to do a girl a favor and she can only find fault." He put his weight on one hip. "Women!"

Lucy opened her mouth to respond but shut it again. He was winding her up. The thought hit her and she was shocked. He was expecting her to react. Her eyes widened as his looked on her, expectant.

Brody Hamilton was using the age-old technique of argument to *flirt*. With her. And, oh, it was tempting to return the favor.

"I thought after the incident with Pretty you would have learned that the way to score points with me isn't to pamper me but to treat me as an equal."

His grin widened at their banter.

"Did you hear that, Bruce?" He looked at the horse and shook his head with mock seriousness. "I think she just insulted your manhood. And here my intentions were pure." He sighed, put upon, and with a chuckle, tilted his head and delivered the final riposte: "Bruce here needs some exercise. And he's pouting because I haven't given him any lately. He thinks senior status entitles him to certain privileges. I thought today I'd make peace by offering him a pretty lady. Perhaps I was wrong."

Lucy's lips twitched. Obviously Mrs. P. had slipped something in Brody's morning coffee because he was cracking jokes and flirting as though all their animosity had never happened. She couldn't help the grin from dawning over her face. Was it so simple as that? That the horse had needed a work-out, and that was Brody's only motivation in choosing him? Perhaps she'd been taking things too personally. She'd been defensive about everything for so long it was second nature. Perhaps it really was as easy as a ride on a summer's day with a cowboy she was starting to like way too much.

"Does that line work for you often?"

He leaned close to the gelding's ear and whispered something, and the horse nudged Brody's shoulder.

"Bruce says not as often as he'd like."

Lucy couldn't help it…she laughed. She wouldn't have guessed that Brody had a play-ful side. She strode up the corridor, carry-ing her cap in her hand. "So what's with the change in mood? You haven't—" she broke off as Brody's left eyebrow lifted. "You haven't seemed very happy I'm here. To put it mildly. Or that I put my oar in about Pret-ty's injury."

Brody came forward, Bruce clopping steadily behind him until he halted right in front of her and handed her the reins.

"I was rude. I'm sorry. I'm not usually that grumpy. Or closed minded."

He actually looked as if he meant it. The

crinkles were gone from the corners of his eyes as he regarded her seriously.

"My word, did I just hear an apology?"

His eyes twinkled. "Must have been the wind."

Bruce was getting impatient and nudged Lucy's shoulder with his head, pushing her toward Brody. It put her off balance and Brody's hands came out to steady her. And stayed, just above her elbows. "Lucy I—" he cleared his throat "—I am sorry. About your mother and about being so rough on you and quick to judge. I'm usually not so hard to get along with."

Her eyes dropped to his lips. They were crisply etched, with a perfect dip in the top one. This was madness. She had to do something to get out of his arms before she did something foolish.

"You're not?"

She raised one brow just a bit in sarcasm, though there was little malice in her now. She'd said it so he'd let her go, but his grip remained firm. They weren't sniping, they were...

She bit down on her lip as she looked up in his eyes. They were *waiting*. Waiting for one of them to make a move. Lucy knew it could never be her. She relaxed her shoulders and took a small step back so he'd let her go. Of all things. Using an aged gelding to set off sparks. She wasn't entirely sure she didn't prefer the nasty Brody. It made distance a heck of a lot easier. Because this Brody—the human, caring one—was a man she'd like to know a lot better. And to do that would mean revealing things about herself she didn't want him to know.

"No, I'm not," he said huskily, his hands still in the air where moments before her arms had been. The intimate tone reached inside her and she wanted to back away. But that would mean letting him win. He would expect her to, and she needed to stand her ground.

"Why were you, then? Why did you judge me so harshly?"

He finally turned away. "Hop on. You're none too tall and your stirrups will need adjusting."

She knew pestering him wouldn't get answers, so she put the hand holding the reins on the saddle horn, her left foot in the stirrup and hopped, sliding into the saddle. Once she was seated she realized that indeed, the stirrups were a few inches too long for her feet.

Brody's hands worked the first buckle and she watched him from above, his strong, capable fingers partially hidden by the brim of his hat.

"Why were you so angry with me?" She repeated the question softly, needing to discover the real reason behind his actions. He could be kind and funny. She wanted to believe that was the real Brody and not the exception. His hands stilled on the leather strap.

"There are just a lot of pressures right now. And…because I don't like people nosing around in my life."

She thought of the discrepancy in the records and knew if she brought it up he'd consider it an invasion of his privacy. And rightly so. How would she feel if he went through her things? He finished the first stirrup and went around to adjust the other.

"Why not? I thought all cowboys were an open book. The uncomplicated type."

He didn't look up at her. She wished he would so she could see his expression. But he kept fiddling with the strap. She relaxed, leaning ahead and resting her hands on the saddle horn.

"I'm not that complicated," he explained. "Doesn't mean life hasn't thrown me complications. Ones that I don't choose to broadcast. Still have to be dealt with, though."

He finally looked up. "Don't you have any of those, Lucy?"

His hand landed on the ankle of her boot and she felt the pressure of it through the leather, connecting them in this one moment. She had so many questions she wanted to ask, and no right to ask them. He wasn't teasing anymore. He wasn't flirting. This went deeper than that. She wanted to reach out and touch his face, just once. To smooth the tiny wrinkle that formed between his eyes, telegraphing his worry.

What could he be dealing with to cause him such distress? Did it have anything to do with when he took over the ranch? Or how his father's signature had suddenly stopped appearing on the official records? But she held back. He was entitled to his secrets as much as she was entitled to hers. And getting too close to him wasn't part of the plan. No matter how good his hand felt. Maybe she needed to know, but this wasn't the way to go about it.

"Then can we agree on one thing, Brody? I'm not here to dig into *your* past. I am only here to forge an alliance, if you will. Between

Prairie Rose and Navarro. Whatever deal we broker should benefit both operations, don't you agree? I was just getting up to speed with records. That's all." She paused. "I didn't go through your files with any other intention than that."

Brody moved away from her leg. "Okay."

"Brody, I…" She swallowed. "Look, I tend to judge on what I see. And, yeah, I also need to know who's running Prairie Rose. It matters. It doesn't mean I need to know every detail."

She met his gaze evenly while Bruce waited patiently for his cue to walk on. Lord, Brody was handsome. More than that, he was steady. She didn't know what he was dealing with, but she knew he'd do it standing tall or not at all. She liked that.

"I'm running Prairie Rose. Just me."

More than ever she wanted to ask about his father, but the words stuck in her mouth. What if he asked about hers?

"I think you're a good man, Brody, and one dedicated to Prairie Rose. That's all I really need to know."

She nudged Bruce and turned him, walking out of the barn into the yard. Maybe that was all she needed to know, but it wasn't all she wanted. She wanted to know about his connections, about his family. Where was his family? Mrs. Polcyk was only a part of it. But she knew that whatever she found out, it was going to have to come from Brody. She wouldn't lower herself to snooping.

Chapter Six

Brody caught up with her a few moments later, riding the bay she'd been hoping to ride herself. It was the first time she'd seen him sit a horse, and he did it with an unmatched naturalness and ease. He was born to be in the saddle. A nearly nonexistent cue from him and the stallion broke into a trot, coming to meet her by the fence.

"Okay, so now I'm jealous."

He flashed a grin at her again, as if the tense moments in the barn hadn't happened. She was beginning to realize that the Brody she wanted to know existed when he was most in his element. He was easier, less guarded. She recognized it because she felt it herself. She got in the saddle and all her troubles seemed to melt away. She could just *be*.

"Ahab's my pride and joy."

It was easy for Lucy to see why. He was tall for a quarter horse—she'd guess at slightly over sixteen hands—with beautifully muscled hindquarters and a broad chest. She remembered the bloodline from the files yesterday—solid. A little mixing of Thoroughbred, which gave him his leaner, taller build. Ahab wasn't a stock horse. At the way his hooves danced impatiently, she knew he'd be agile and fast. Exactly what Navarro was looking for, exactly as her father had said. But at the look on Brody's face, she knew. "He's not for sale, then."

Brody patted Ahab's neck. "Nope. Not for sale." He inclined his chin at a field ahead. "You wanna head out?"

"Why not? Though I doubt Bruce and I will be able to keep up."

"Don't underestimate Bruce. He's got a competitive heart."

Brody nudged Ahab into a canter and Lucy followed, letting out all her pent-up oxygen in a rush as Brody led her out of the lane and into a meadow. She watched him from be-

hind. Perhaps Ahab wasn't for sale, but she
definitely wanted to talk to Brody about stud
fees. He was far and away the finest piece of
horseflesh she'd seen in months. But it wasn't
just Ahab. It was Brody. Yes, he was a pain in
the neck. He was also dead sexy. Definitely a
complication she didn't need. She had an obligation to fulfil. She'd promised King Alexander that she'd do this job properly, and that
meant going back to Marazur and…

She frowned. And what? Taking her place
as princess? Is that what Alexander had
planned for her? It didn't seem possible. And
it was the last thing she wanted to think about
on a beautiful morning like this.

She nudged Bruce along, only slightly behind Brody, and her chest expanded in the
clear air. This was what she'd missed over the
past week. In the few days before leaving she
hadn't had any time to escape. Now, with the
warm summer breeze in her face and the familiar rocking motion of Bruce beneath her,
the stress she'd been holding on to dissipated
into the prairie breeze. They rode for several
minutes in silence, following the fence line
north, up over a small knoll and toward a thin
line of trees in the distance.

Brody stayed slightly ahead with Ahab,

which was fine with Lucy. She was more than enjoying the freedom and wide-open space. The sky here was so huge, like a giant blue ceiling that went on far beyond the walls of her vision. There was room here, in the drying grasses and the calls of the birds and the gentle hills. There was room to simply exist. There was a wild freedom here she hadn't experienced in a long time. Like spring-cleaning day when her mother had thrown open all the doors and windows and let the sunshine and fresh air in. It almost felt like a new beginning. But that was silly. She'd had all the new beginnings she'd care to have for a long time. For a fleeting moment she almost wished she were back in Marazur, running the stable and keeping a low profile at the palace. There was only so much change a girl could take. At least there she knew what the expectations were. Here, at Prairie Rose, they constantly seemed to change with Brody's mood.

Brody turned along a fence line and she caught sight of several horses grazing below. She kept trying to puzzle him out. The very first day he'd been teasing with her, and then almost angry when he realized who she was. She wondered if it had to do with her, or if it was just because she was there and digging into his past. She didn't like the twist he put on the nickname "princess," either. She was sure he hadn't realized the truth of her identity, but that didn't stop the resentment and guilt she felt whenever he used it, even if it was in jest.

Brody slowed Ahab to a walk and halted. As she came closer, she saw him relax in the curve of the saddle, lean his head back and let the sun warm his face. With utter fascination she slowed Bruce to a walk and watched as Brody took a deep breath and let it out.

This was why she cared. She understood what that breath meant. There was something about Prairie Rose, something about being here and being with the horses that she recognized and responded to. She'd tried to capture the same freedom in Marazur but had failed. Every time she tried to sneak away for a ride on the cliffs, King Alexander had security follow her. She supposed it was his idea of being an attentive father. But there was no one here now. She was *free*.

Prairie Rose Ranch was different, yet much the same as the life she remembered. She could tell Brody felt the same bone-deep appreciation for it. The gorgeousness of a summer sun soaking through a T-shirt. The pungent warmth of horse and worn leather, the wide-open space and the something that was elemental about all of it brought a catch to her chest. What would it be like to be here all the time? To be a part of a ranch like Prairie Rose? To be with Brody? She licked her lips. Perhaps it would be easier to imagine if she could figure him out.

She came up beside him and stopped, looping the reins over the horn and turning her face to the sun, as well.

"I'd had you pegged as an English girl, princess."

Eyes closed, she chuckled softly. There wasn't any derision in his use of the name this time, only teasing.

"Naw, Western. When I was eight years old my mum finally decided something had to be done with me and asked if I could take lessons at the Oak. I did a lot of western pleasure riding, right up to my teens. Once I started working, though..."

"You?" he prompted. He turned in the saddle to look at her, eyes curious. She opened her eyes and caught him staring.

"I'd been hanging around the stables for years, first riding, then helping the grooms.

I started working part-time in high school and then got more involved. The owner was dabbling in racing a bit and I wanted more action. I changed my manners and discipline for speed."

"You surprise me."

She looked over at him as a crow cawed in the trees ahead. "By the time Mum got sick, I was assistant manager."

"Then why did you leave?" Brody shifted in the saddle, the leather squeaking softly.

Lucy couldn't meet his eyes. So many choices to make about what truths to tell and yet…talking with Brody today and in the barn the other night helped her feel more connected to herself than she had in a long, long time. "I made a promise to my mother. She wanted me to explore other areas of my life. I promised her I would. I can't go back on that promise. It…"

But she broke off, suddenly grieving again. She hadn't realized what a grounding force her mum had been when she'd been alive. And now she was gone and had taken Lucy's touchstone with her. How Lucy wished her mum could be there to talk to now. Lucy could have apologized for the things she'd said at the end. Things she would always regret.

But if her mother had still been alive, Lucy wouldn't have gone to Marazur. She wouldn't even be at Prairie Rose. Funny how things worked out. She wasn't even sure if it was a good or a bad thing. And she still felt guilty for going to Marazur in the first place. To get away from her mother and from the lies. She'd been so angry. At her mother for lying. At her mother for getting sick. And even at Alexander for making no demands on her at all. It was almost as if he didn't quite care what she did. He was so perfectly agreeable she felt completely useless. Redundant.

"I know about making promises. Even when they're tough ones. She'd be happy you are following through with it, Lucy."

Lucy turned tear-filled eyes to him. She remembered her mother telling her about Alexander and then revealing that she'd invited him to come to the States to see her. The words Lucy had said…she couldn't take them back. And when she'd told them—together— that she was dying, all Lucy had been able to feel was anger and helplessness and she'd lashed out about being manipulated. She'd apologized, but the words could never be taken back. When her mother had made her promise to go to Marazur, she couldn't refuse. The day after the funeral she'd actually been glad to get away.

"It was all she ever asked of me. I couldn't very well refuse her."

Brody saw the tears and wanted to reach out and hold her, like he had in the barn. It wasn't her fault he was angry. He'd been angry for so long, he almost forgot what it was like to be anything else. And yet…there were times when he caught himself teasing her and wondered how she'd snuck past his guard. He didn't want to care. It would only complicate things.

"I'm sorry about your mother, Lucy."

She brushed away her tears with the back of her free hand. "I didn't mean to get weepy. You brought me out here for a ride and here I am getting all girly on you."

Girly, indeed. Because he couldn't help but notice the dusting of freckles over her nose or the way her firm breasts looked in a plain T-shirt. There was something more natural about Lucy today. A princess? Hardly, but no less alluring. Her unruly red curls were pulled back and tucked through the hole at the back of her cap. Her jeans were faded, as though she'd worn them often, and her T-shirt was tan-colored, making her pale skin look even paler. Delicate.

Damn.

That line of thinking would only get him in trouble. She was here to do a job. And today he felt better about her—at least in a professional capacity. She'd been honest with him about her purpose, and then she'd demonstrated that she wasn't just another flunkie sent to analyze charts and records. She *was* a horsewoman. Only someone who knew what they were about could have picked up on Pretty's injury. He'd like to think he would have noticed right off but wasn't sure.

He looked at her long fingers, the leather reins threaded through them and longed to touch them, to reassure her it would be okay. Feeling drawn to her wasn't right, but he'd wanted her with him today anyway. She'd earned the right to see the rest of the ranch, and he'd needed the break himself. Going into town yesterday hadn't been fun, and he was glad she hadn't pressed him about where he was going. Details. Details that needed attention and that reminded him of how much responsibility he had. And Lucy somehow reminded him that there was more to life than endless responsibility. He could say that it was part of the job, showing her around. But the truth of the matter was, he'd needed to escape for a while and he'd wanted to do it with her.

He'd wondered if the rolling prairie would bore her, but she looked free and happy. He recognized that look. It wasn't one he wore very often, but today, playing hooky and going for a joy ride reminded him of why Prairie Rose was a labor of love rather than obligation.

He had enough obligation to worry about, anyway. And right now that didn't include making eyes at Lucy Farnsworth. It certainly didn't include the crazy thought that she looked *right* sitting there astride Bruce. Like she belonged. Again he was reminded of how he'd thought that once before, only to be proved completely wrong. Things weren't always as they seemed. Lisa had taught him that.

He swallowed the bitter taste in his mouth and nodded toward the trees. "You want to see the old homestead?"

She nodded, but he heard the telltale sniff that she tried to hide. Her feelings were still raw. Her mother hadn't been gone that long.

He remembered how that felt, how the moments snuck up on you when you realized everything had changed forever.

He tried a teasing smile, hoping to cajole her out of her doldrums. "I'll race you."

Before he could blink, she'd dug her heels into Bruce and set off down the hill, her head low over his neck. At his signal, Ahab leaped forward, his long stride stretching over the tall grass. She shoved her hat further over her eyes and bent low, urging him on, her knees tight against the saddle as her laughter danced back to him on the wind. With a whoop, he gave Ahab free rein. They caught Bruce and Lucy halfway and galloped side by side the rest of the distance, the bright sound of their laughter chasing them.

They pulled up in a pouf of dust at the border of trees around a small dilapidated building. Lucy walked Bruce forward, turned him by a poplar tree and brought him back, both of them winded. Her grin was wide and free, and Brody let the answering laughter come, let it feel good after months of it being a stranger. "I guess you were right. Bruce didn't stand a chance."

Lucy's breath came in bursts of exertion. "Yes, but Bruce has got a valiant heart, don't you, sweetheart." She leaned forward and pressed a kiss to his gray, damp hide. Bruce halted beside Ahab, so that she was face-to-face with Brody.

She sat up and lifted the brim of her ball cap a bit. "What is this place?"

Brody smiled again, more at ease than he'd expected to be. Lord, she was beautiful. And not in any flashy, extravagant way. There was something so natural about her. She reminded him of the flower that was the ranch's name-sake. A wild rose. Beautiful, but in a take-me-as-I-am, unostentatious way. Her hair set off the creaminess of her skin. He touched the tip of his finger to her nose. "The sun is making you freckle."

He had touched her without thinking, and shifted in the saddle as her lips dropped open with surprise.

"Sorry," he muttered, and slid out of the saddle, putting his back to her. Stupid, stupid. Noticing her *skin,* of all things!

Her laugh floated on the breeze behind him. "I'm embarrassingly pasty for some-one who lives in the Mediterranean. Blame it on my Irish roots—red hair and pale skin. But I burn easily, so the secret is SPF a zil-lion. Apparently today I missed my nose."

He imagined her smoothing the lotion over her arms and swallowed thickly.

He narrowed his eyes. Her reference to her home reminded him that she was only here to do a job and she'd be leaving in a matter of days. He'd do better to remember that she was here at the request of the king of Marazur and stop weaving fancies that didn't exist. She didn't belong here. She had no idea what Prairie Rose was really about. She certainly wouldn't have found it in the files from yesterday. Or even with Bill and Arnie and Pretty.

"This is a sod house, isn't it!" Curious, Lucy made her way through the weeds to the small structure. She turned her head briefly to look at him, and his heart constricted.

Yeah, he was testing her. He'd forgotten that in the joy of racing, but her remark about Marazur reminded him. He'd figured she'd bear out his expectations and that'd be that. Lisa had taken one look at the soddy and had turned up her nose, laughing. She'd wondered why they'd kept it, a pile of dirt in the middle of the prairie. But Lucy was looking at him as if he'd given her a precious gem, when the reality was that it was just like Lisa had said. A mound of dirt in the middle of nowhere.

It would have been easier if she, too, had turned her nose up at it, rather than looking at it with such interest.

She stepped gingerly around the structure, peering in through the opening where the door once was. "Who lived here, Brody?"

He stepped forward, unable to keep from recounting the story. It was one his mother had told him often after his grandmother had passed on.

"My great-great-grandparents. They settled this land in the late nineteenth century. And lived in a soddy as they built it up and raised beef."

"Can you imagine living here? My God, the hardship." Her voice came from around the other side, and he looked toward where the sound came from. All he could see was waving grass and scrub brush. Her voice came, hollow on the wind as she circled the structure. "We complain when the power goes out for a few hours. And they lived and loved each other right here in a home made of dirt and grass."

She reappeared on the other side, her smile wide. "Amazing, isn't it! You must be so proud."

"Proud?" Proud, of a family that was poor

as church mice? Of a family who'd been foolish enough to lose so much? He looked away.
There was no distaste in her eyes, just curiosity. He'd wondered, considering she now
lived in such luxury. But Lucy *got* this place.
He could see it in her. The way she valued
roots, the way she talked about her mother
and Trembling Oak. And he'd been prepared
for her to turn up her nose.

"Of course, proud! Think of how strong
they must have been to stick it out. Not just
here, but with each other. Marriage is…"

She broke off the sentence and looked uncomfortable. He tried to meet her gaze but
she averted her eyes. "Marriage is…?"

His heart pounded. She couldn't know
about Lisa. He'd said absolutely nothing to
make her suspect he'd been married before,
and he doubted Mrs. P. would have, either.
The subject of his failed marriage was a
no-go zone.

"I was just going to say that marriage is
difficult enough without throwing hardships
into the mix."

Throw in a few hardships and marriage
did get difficult. Too difficult. He knew that
all too well.

"And you're basing this on…?"

Brody shoved his hands in his pockets but he didn't waste time waiting for an answer. "Have you been married, Lucy? What about your mum? You've mentioned her before, but not your dad. I take it that wasn't a happy family unit, either."

She angled her head, watching him closely. He didn't like the way she was looking at him. As if she was on the verge of asking questions he didn't want to answer.

"I didn't know my dad, growing up."

"Really. So they were divorced?"

This time Lucy looked away. "My mum and dad split up when I was a baby."

Brody ignored the little voice inside him that said he was pressing too much. "Do you even know who he is?"

Lucy's nostrils flared. He'd touched a nerve, apparently. Good. He'd heard enough about what everyone thought had caused *his* marriage to fall apart, when he knew the truth: Lisa hadn't loved him. She'd loved something she'd thought he was, and when it wasn't true she'd cut and run. Fast.

"I do know my father, yes. Though you're really being an insulting ass right now."

"And is he married?" He kept on, undeterred.

Lucy's eyes snapped and her cheeks turned red. "Why does it matter?"

Brody snorted. "All this makes you a judge of marriage, I suppose? You didn't grow up with one and you haven't experienced it yourself."

She stepped away from the soddy and came closer. "You don't need to get run over by a tractor to know it's gonna hurt," she remarked, stepping over a large stone. She stopped in front of him. "People can imagine themselves in situations, good and bad, and have something of an understanding of what it would be like."

"Really."

Lucy let out a growl of frustration. "Honestly, Brody, you change direction more than the wind out here. You're joking and happy one moment, and an absolute bear the next. Haven't you ever imagined something wonderful and you knew exactly what it would be like without having experienced it?"

His gaze dropped to her lips and stuck there. Yeah, he had. Because right now he was imagining what it would be like to kiss her. To taste the sunlight on her lips and hear her sigh against him. To touch that silky-soft skin of her arms as he held her close.

Was she right? Was he really that miserable? It was true he'd felt the strain of running everything single-handedly more the last few years. And he didn't trust easily. But had he really become so crotchety?

"You might want to get back on that horse and head on home," he muttered, unable to tear his eyes away from her mouth.

"Why? Because you're going to snap at me again? Insult me and my family?" She puffed out a derisive breath. "By now I'm almost immune."

"Damn it, Lucy…"

She laughed at him then, and it made him so mad he could only act. He grabbed the brim of her cap, pulling it off her head and sending the gingery curls springing around her face. Her lips dropped open in shock the moment he dropped the cap on the ground and shoved his hands into the rippling mass. The surprise in her eyes was instantly replaced with something new. Passion. Desire. He let it feed him as he tilted her head back and pressed his mouth to hers.

Lucy's hands hung limply at her sides momentarily as Brody's lips hit hers, not asking but demanding a response. His mouth was firm and hot and very, very agile. She lifted her hands and pressed the fingertips into his shoulders, standing on tiptoe and finally curling her fingers around the back of his neck. He teased her mouth open wider and tilted his head, the brim of his hat shading them both from the glaring sun.

He eased off, nipping her bottom lip between his teeth, and all her nerve endings shot to her core. She put her weight back on her heels as his hands withdrew from her hair, leaving the curls in a wild mess.

"You were wrong." His voice was gravelly, and a shiver went through her despite the heat.

"Wrong about…" she squeaked, cleared her throat, and started again. "Wrong about what?"

"You can imagine things all you want, but they're rarely what you expect."

Her cheeks flushed. The insult was clear. She'd just made a complete fool of herself. Crawling all over him as if he was irresistible. A magpie cackled in a nearby poplar, taunting her.

He had kissed *her,* she reminded herself, not the other way around. He'd been the one to pick a fight. He was the one who kept changing his mind. She'd been the one to keep her head—for the most part. She lifted her chin.

"You, Brody Hamilton, are mean." She wasn't about to let anyone play her for a fool, not again. "You did that deliberately. Well, congratulations on proving your point. You can go on being miserable, just the way you like it."

The last word broke but she didn't care. She picked up her cap out of the dust and shook it off. "From now on let's just talk about your stock, shall we? I'll start putting together a proposal based on what I've seen and we can talk fees. That's what I came for, and that's what I'm taking back with me."

"Where are you going?"

She glared at him with one foot in the stirrup. "You'll have to find someone else to argue with, it wasn't in my job description." Tears of humiliation pricked the backs of her eyelids. She slid into the saddle and shoved her hair haphazardly through the cap once more.

Then she spun Bruce around and urged him into a gallop, flying over the prairie, heading back to the barns.

Brody Hamilton had played her for a fool. She was relieved she hadn't told him the truth after all. Right now all she wanted to do was do her job! And then catch the first flight home.

Bruce rebelled at the pace and she relaxed, letting him slow down. Home. It struck her that she'd just referred to Marazur as home. How had that happened?

Chapter Seven

For two days Brody and Lucy maintained a cold, polite relationship that consisted of examining stock and negotiating stud fees. No more insults, no more joking, and definitely no more kissing.

Never would Lucy have imagined herself wishing to go back to Marazur and the palace. She was only there because of guilt and promises to begin with, and because she had known in her heart it was a wonderful opportunity professionally. She certainly hadn't taken the job out of loyalty to her father.

Her mother had waited until almost the end before telling her about Alexander, and then had used her illness to make Lucy promise to go to Marazur. Alexander had come, and Mary Ellen had told them both what the doctors had told her—that she was terminal. She hadn't wanted Lucy left alone. And at Lucy's resistance, she'd then pointed out Navarro's reputation and that she had to think of her future. Lucy had promised, too afraid to do anything else. But Lucy had said things… awful things…to Alexander. And her mother had heard every hurtful word.

Lucy sighed and sipped her coffee. The dew still lay thick on the grass and a cluster of ducks flapped overhead, flying toward the pond beyond the barns. Despite all she'd said, Alexander had still asked her to come. He'd still entrusted her with his prized stables. And he'd trusted her to do this job. She couldn't imagine why. She'd heard him all but admit to her half brother, Raoul, that he was at a loss as to what to do with her. But then he'd sent her here, and he would never have done that if he didn't think she was capable of it. He took his stables too seriously.

It was Saturday, and back in Virginia she'd be putting in a half day with the horses and then likely going out with friends for the evening.

Not today. Today she was stuck at Prairie

Rose wondering about Brody. Not very productive.

"Lucy?"

Brody's voice stirred her and she took her feet off the empty chair and put them back on the deck floor.

"Yes?"

"I'm going into town later this morning. Thought maybe you'd like to come. See civilization, such as it is."

It was a polite invitation. He probably didn't even mean it; Mrs. Polcyk had probably put him up to it. But it might be a chance for her to do something nice for the housekeeper who had brokered a peace between them for the past few days. They'd have hardly spoken at all if Mrs. P. hadn't been there urging things along.

"Is Mrs. P. coming?"

"No, she's got a bit of a summer cold and she's taking it easy."

Lucy turned around in her chair. Brody was standing by the sliding door, neither smiling nor frowning. Waiting for her answer.

Brody was holding secrets. And it wasn't like he was going to sit down and have a big heart-to-heart with her, now, was it? Curiosity bubbled inside her. Since he'd lived here all his life, maybe she'd be able to put some pieces together by going to Larch Valley with him. Get some answers. If there was news about Prairie Rose, a community this small would surely know about it.

"I might like that. If Mrs. P. puts together a list, I can pick things up for her."

"That's generous of you."

Silence fell, uncomfortable.

"Lucy, I…"

"Brody…"

He stepped out on the deck, his hat in his hands. "I was way out of line the other day. I was deliberately insulting and hurtful. I'm not usually. My mama would kick my behind to know I'd spoken to a woman that way."

Her lips curved the faintest bit. Ah, mothers. Did they have any idea how much power they exerted even after they were gone? She thought of her own mother. Where was Brody's? But the peace between them was too tentative for her to ask. She looked into his eyes. He seemed earnest.

And she realized he was apologizing for what he'd said, not about what he'd done. Her heart fluttered. She was finding it difficult to regret the kiss, too, even if she had failed his test. It had been a long time since she'd been kissed like that.

"We seem to goad each other without even trying."

"We've both had a lot on our minds, I think."

Lucy thought for a moment. She knew what her problem was. She was angry. She wanted something she didn't have and she was downright mad about it. Maybe he was angry, too. Maybe he'd never planned his life to be this way. The paperwork showed he'd taken control of the ranch several years ago, but no inkling why. She couldn't presume to be the only one with hurts and regrets. What regret did he hold inside?

"You want to talk about it, Brody? About why you're so angry?"

She tilted her head back so she could see him properly, raising her eyebrows.

"Not really. You?"

She thought about just saying, *Hey Brody, my dad's really King Alexander of Marazur but I didn't know that until three months ago.* And she nearly laughed at what she imagined his expression would be, especially given the nickname he'd dubbed her with. She had to give her father credit. He'd seen her unhappiness and had sent her here. She'd gotten the impression it was to placate her, but she was determined to go back and show her worth, to exceed his expectations. She didn't want to be simply Princess Luciana. She wanted a place she'd earned.

And to do that, she had to earn Brody's approval first.

"Nope. I'm not really a sharing type of girl, if you haven't noticed."

He chuckled. "So let's take a day off from being mad and from working. I have some errands to run, and I'm going in, anyway. You might as well come with me. There's a farmer's market and some shops for you to visit if you like."

"That sounds nice."

"I'd like to leave in an hour."

"I'll be ready."

He slid the door shut behind him and she went back to her coffee.

Larch Valley was exactly what Lucy expected from a small western town. A little like stepping back in time, with the stores still sporting false fronts, and antique-style streetlamps along Main Avenue. She looked out the window of Brody's half-ton truck and smiled. Here was a place where children played in the park before being called home to supper and you'd get your week's worth of gossip at the local hairdressers on a morning such as this.

"I can drop you off here, if you like. Follow the avenue down to the end for the market. There are shops all along here, though. If that's okay."

She looked over at him as he pulled up to the curb. His lips were thinned and tense and she wondered why. What was he doing in town today that caused him to be so uptight? Was it personal or business? He'd already been to town once this week. Her mind raced back to the file she'd mulled over, sensing something wasn't right but not able to put her finger on it.

"I could come with you. I don't mind waiting."

He turned his head away from her and stared out the windshield. "You'd be bored to death."

She didn't want to pick another fight, not when they had such a tenuous truce going. She'd have to find her answers elsewhere. "Okay. I'll meet you at the market then?"

"In about an hour."

She opened the truck door and hopped out. He gave a wave of his hand, but still wasn't smiling as he drove off. It definitely wasn't an errand he was looking forward to.

She glanced around her. The avenue *was* quaint. Across the street was a small gazebo, bordered with some sort of weeping tree…one she'd never seen before. The bark reminded her of birch, but the leaves were tiny and hung toward the ground like silvery green curtains. A group of children played soccer in a small area, their shoes trampling the grass. It was lush and green—obviously watered, because on the drive in, most of the fields had been dry and brown in the late-August climate.

She turned her attention to the sidewalk before her and smiled. In Virginia they'd always been close to Norfolk and now in Marazur… she was used to urban centers.

She'd never been one for small towns really. But Larch Valley was pretty in its quiet, take-me-as-I-am way. All along Main Avenue, iron and wood benches waited to be occupied in the summer sun. Baskets of gaily painted petunias and lobelia hung from the streetlamps, and urns of geraniums sat near doorsteps or beamed from window boxes.

Brody had been in this town his whole life. He'd probably gone to school here. She thought about it for a moment. He'd probably had girlfriends from here. Girls he'd known his whole life.

She frowned, surprised at her own line of thinking. She began to wander down the concrete walk. It shouldn't matter to her about Brody's love life. There was nothing between them. There couldn't be.

She sat heavily on a bench. This was silly. She had a fantastic job, money in her pocket. Lived in a palace. So why was she unhappy? And why did suddenly walking down a street in Larch Valley make her feel as though she was coming home? She'd never been here before. She didn't belong. Brody had made that clear the other day at the soddy.

No, in a few short days she'd be going back to Marazur. And if Alexander was happy with her performance, she'd be in charge of one of the most successful Thoroughbred racing stables in Europe. It was what she wanted. It was her way of subtly thumbing her nose at her father, to show him she'd done just fine without him. She'd go back and show him she was worthy of the job. This sort of position had been her goal as long as she could remember.

Except, back in Marazur there wouldn't be any Brody.

She covered her eyes with a hand. She shouldn't be thinking about Brody. Not after one disastrous kiss. It couldn't be Brody's fault. It was this place. It did funny things to her, that was all.

She got up and continued down the street, fighting the weird sense of familiarity, stopping before a white door. It was opened partway, and delicious smells wafted out: cinnamon and fruit and bread all mingled together. She knew what was on her shopping list, but she couldn't resist the urge to buy a treat.

The bell above the door tinkled as she pushed it the rest of the way open. "Be right with you!" came a shout from somewhere in the back of the building. Within seconds, a red-faced woman bearing a tray of buns bustled in.

"Morning! Sorry about that." Her hands flew as she arranged the buns behind the glass counter. "What can I get you?" she asked, straightening and dusting off her hands.

Lucy smiled. "Something that tastes as good as it smells in here."

The woman flashed a grin. "I'm afraid you'll have to be more specific."

Lucy laughed. "I was afraid you'd say that."

The woman couldn't have been more than thirty, Lucy realized, and she wondered how on earth she'd managed to stay so slim surrounded by sweet treats and breads all day. "Chocolate. I'd like something chocolate."

"Brownies. Made them first thing this morning and iced 'em hot." The woman pulled a pan out from a steel rack behind her. "I haven't even put them out yet."

Lucy could smell them—moist, rich chocolate. Her stomach turned over. Today had been coffee and a slice of toast for breakfast. She was already imagining a slab of brownie with a glass of cold milk.

She wondered if Brody liked brownies.

"I'll take them...and..." She paused. Maybe it would be silly to ask.

"And?"

"Do you know Brody Hamilton?" she blurted out.

The woman laughed. "'Course I do. Everyone knows Brody."

And Lucy felt that damnable blush heat her cheeks again.

"Oh," the woman said. Her smile grew.

"Oh, no," replied Lucy quickly. "It's not… no. I mean, I just should've known you knew him. It being a small town and all."

The woman handed over the brownies and raised an eyebrow.

"I mean…" Lord, she sounded like an idiot. She supposed that asking about Brody like a besotted fool would look less like she was prying. Yet she was at a loss as to what questions to ask. "I'm staying at Prairie Rose on business, and Brody brought me into town. I told Mrs. Polcyk I'd pick up a few things, seeing as she's not feeling well…"

"Betty's under the weather?"

The interruption didn't surprise her nearly as much as the use of Mrs. P.'s first name. "Uh, yes. She's got a bit of a cold."

The young woman's brow creased. "That woman, working too hard again." Her hands flew once more as she put a selection of items in a paper bag. "I'm sending you some herb bread and a bag of buns. You stop at the market and pick up some sausage, even if it's not on the list. It's Betty's favorite."

Lucy wasn't put off by the order; it amused

her. This was a place where everyone looked after each other, it seemed. She blinked. Why was it, then, that Brody seemed to feel responsible for everyone else and so bent on doing things himself? He'd mentioned obligation. It made her wonder. What sort of obligation was he under?

"One last thing," she said lightly, her heart pounding like a schoolgirl's. "Do you know if Brody has any favorites? Mrs. Polcyk always seems to be baking, and it would be nice if she didn't have to, for once."

A pie box was added to the bag with the brownies. "How well do you know Brody again?"

She would not blush. She would not.

"I'm just visiting from another stable. That's all."

"I see." She rang up the total, and Lucy paid the bill. "Well, you tell Brody that Jen says hi, and that he'd better save me a dance at his barn dance next Saturday."

Jen? A dance?

She swallowed, smiled as her mind raced. "I'll do that. Thanks."

Outside she breathed the morning air and wondered who Jen was to Brody and what dance she was talking about. It didn't matter. Lucy would likely be gone by then, anyway. She adjusted the bags in her arms and lifted her head. She'd just make her way to the market and wait to meet Brody. She'd done enough of being silly this morning. If she had questions she should just come out and ask him herself. She didn't have much time, she might as well wander and explore. She wouldn't have time for it again before she left.

On the way to the market she couldn't help but be charmed. People on the street nodded hello; a couple of old men sat outside a diner and drank coffee, gesturing with their hands as they debated. Children sat on benches outside the ice cream parlour, licking cones that were melting in the warm morning sun. She was almost to the market when a sign caught her attention—Agnes's Antiques.

She went inside.

It was a treasure trove of items, from the flea-market quality to true finds. Old cola paraphernalia next to gorgeous willowware dishes. Sepia pictures and handmade dolls in nearly new condition.

"Hello, dear."

The woman was Agnes. There was no possibility of her being anyone else, Lucy concluded. Her gray hair was pulled precisely to the back of her head in a tight bun, and little glasses sat on her nose. Her eyes were sharp as tacks and Lucy, short, petite Lucy, felt somehow large and ungainly.

"Anything I can help you find?"

"I'm just looking, thank you."

Agnes came forward. "Why don't you let me take those bags for you. Wouldn't want you bumping into things."

She reminded Lucy of an old schoolteacher she'd once had. Kind, but oh, so particular. She put the bags on the counter and smiled. "I'm new to the area and was passing by."

"Of course. You're the young lady staying out at Prairie Rose."

Lucy's lips dropped open. "How did you know that?"

Agnes's eyes twinkled. "Small town, dear. News travels."

Lucy found she didn't mind the intrusion. In some small way it made her feel as though she belonged.

"Prairie Rose is lovely. I haven't had time to get much into its history though." She ignored the guilt sneaking through her at the obvious prodding. "I did gather from Brody that it's been in the family a long time."

Agnes smiled. "Oh, yes. Not always quarter horses, mind you. That was John's idea—Brody's dad. He was a real horseman through and through. I taught him in elementary school, you know."

Lucy smiled widely. So she had been right—a schoolteacher. She had that look and way about her.

Agnes beckoned with a finger. "Come and see this. You might find it interesting, seeing as how you're out at the ranch."

Lucy followed her through the dim store to the back, where Agnes took a picture down from a hook. "This isn't really an antique, but it sure is about history." She smiled. "That's Brody." She pointed to a small dark-haired boy in a miniature cowboy hat. It seemed he always wore one, even then. Lucy smiled at the image of him. He couldn't have been more than four years old. "And this here's his mum, Irene, and dad, John, and Hal and Betty Polcyk. Of course this was way before…"

Her face dimmed as she sighed.

"Before?" Lucy tore her eyes away from the picture and looked at Agnes.

Agnes peered over her glasses. "Woulda thought Brody had mentioned it. His mum, dad and the Polcyks were in an accident several years ago. Irene and Hal were killed."

"And his dad?"

Agnes took the picture from her hands and hung it on the hook again. "Oh, he's still at the nursing home. But it took Brody a long time to get things right at Prairie Rose after everything that had gone wrong. Boy darn near worked himself to the bone. But then," she peered over her glasses at Lucy, "men have been doing that in this part of the country for years. Ranching's hard work. Brody knew that and he's done a fine job putting things right."

An accident and the nursing home? Lucy had so many questions she wanted to ask, but not of Agnes. She wanted to ask Brody what the woman meant when she said putting things right. She wanted to know why he never mentioned the accident, or that he had any family at all. She'd shared bits and pieces with him, perhaps not a whole truth but parts of herself, yet he'd backed away when she'd asked a simple question about his parents. She wanted to know why he'd neglected to mention a father that apparently lived...

It clicked into place. Here. His father lived

here. Brody had taken over Prairie Rose. And there was the gap.

At her silence Agnes peered at her with hawklike eyes. "You just go ahead and browse around, dear, and if you have any questions, ask."

Lucy had plenty of questions, and still another twenty minutes before she would meet Brody at the market. Mrs. P.'s husband, Brody's father, Brody's mother. Where had Brody been? And was Mrs. P. the only one who'd gotten out in one piece? Was she the only family Brody had left? Her heart ached for what he must have gone through.

She wandered through the store, thinking back to the two days she'd spent going over files. Brody had mentioned he'd bought Pretty seven years ago—his first solo purchase. She'd just taken it as a sign that Brody had assumed control as sons were wont to do. But now she got the feeling there was something more. Something had gone wrong, and she wanted to know what. And this time it had nothing to do with protecting the Navarro's interests. She wanted to know about Brody. Perhaps if she stayed on a few more days...

She stopped before a clothing rack, a mot-

ley selection of vintage blouses and dresses
and skirts. Her eyes fell on a long skirt in
navy. She reached out and touched it, realiz-
ing the stitching was done by hand. The tiny
stitches were fine, intricate and exact. Every
seam lay flat in the fitted waist, then flowed
out toward the hem. Agnes had paired it
with a blue flowered blouse...complete with
fine white satin fringe along the breast and
mother-of-pearl buttons.

"Gorgeous, isn't it." The older woman's
voice came from behind her. "Been here for
ages. Used to belong to Mathilda Brown. She
did lots of rodeoin' in her day. And, land,
could that girl dance. She was the belle of
the Stampede during the war."

Lucy reluctantly let go of the fringe and
turned. Even coming from Virginia, she
knew all about the Calgary Stampede. "The
Greatest Outdoor Show on Earth," she
quoted, gratified when Agnes smiled.

"That'd just about fit you, you know."

Lucy looked at it longingly. For years
there'd been little money for extravagance,
and buying a vintage outfit certainly qualified. But now she didn't need to be concerned
about money. She smiled. She could afford
to do this now. And perhaps someday when

she was back in Marazur she could put it on and remember her time here. Could pretend to be Mathilda Brown and feel the skirt flirt with her calves as she danced…

Danced. What would it be like to dance with Brody? She remembered the feel of his hard chest against hers as he'd pulled her close to kiss her. So hard, yet so very gentle, too. What if what Jen said was correct? Was there a dance? If she stayed on a few days, she would be able to go.

She wanted to be with him again. To see his eyes fall on her the way they had in the barn that first night, to feel his lips on hers as they had at the soddy. It wasn't rational and it wasn't smart, but it was what she wanted. She wanted to be able to take that bit of him with her.

"I'll take it."

Agnes beamed. "Oh, you'll look lovely in it." Her keen eyes peered over the frames of her glasses. "And I hear the annual dance out at Prairie Rose is next weekend. Perfect time to try it out."

Lucy smiled at the older woman warmly. "That's the general idea."

Agnes took the outfit from Lucy's hands and bustled behind the cash register to wrap it. "Of course, the former Mrs. Hamilton would never have worn such a thing, but I think it's just right."

"Mrs. Hamilton?" Lucy puckered her brow. "Why not?" Lucy looked at the navy skirt again. It was very traditional, very western. Not that she knew much about Brody's mother, but somehow it just seemed to *fit* with Prairie Rose.

"Oh, she was too fine for this sort of thing. Always felt sorry for Brody, though. Lots of head shaking happened when that wife of his left him for greener pastures when things got sticky."

Lucy's hand froze on her purse. Not his mother, as she'd thought.

Wife. He had been married.

Suddenly his hot-and-cold moods made perfect sense. The way he looked at her as if she'd made some grievous mistake, and then at other times as though there was something more. Clearly he wasn't over his ex-wife. All these days…and it hadn't been about her at all. It had been about his wife.

Knowing it cut into her far more deeply than it should have.

After all she'd learned today, she knew that Brody had to be hurt by his past. And if he knew the truth about her it would only pain him further. And yet…she still wanted that dance. One chance to be held in his arms, in Mathilda Brown's skirt and fringe.

Staying at Prairie Rose permanently wasn't an option; there was no reason for her to. Brody didn't need a stable manager and he certainly wasn't in love with her, nor would he ever be. A weight settled in her stomach. If he wasn't over his wife, he certainly wouldn't acknowledge any feelings for Lucy. And she did want to prove her mettle to her father, which meant resuming her position at Navarro. But a dance with him…would be a lovely memory to take back to Marazur. Something to hold on to.

She checked her watch. In only a few moments, Brody would be expecting her, and she would pick up what Mrs. Polcyk had requested. She thanked Agnes and put the bag with her other purchases, hurrying out the door.

And saw Brody's truck turning out of a parking lot on to Third Street and coming in her direction.

She hurried to the entrance of the market just as he was finding a parking spot. When he came around the hood of the truck, she noticed the lines in his face had deepened. It made her want to reach out and smooth them, to ask him what put them there and try to make it better. To tell him that whoever she was had been a fool to walk away and leave him to deal with everything all alone.

She couldn't fathom why she cared so deeply. The last few days he had been merely polite. He'd all but come out and said that her kiss hadn't been up to scratch.

The problem was, his had been. And she wanted the chance to try again. In the skirt and blouse she'd just bought.

"I'm sorry I'm late. I haven't even been inside."

He eyed her packages. "But you have been shopping."

"Well, yes." She lifted one arm slightly, putting a paper bag into relief. "I couldn't resist the bakery and then the antique shop."

His lips barely moved, though she got a glimpse of what might have been a smile. "Jen there this morning?"

She ignored the spurt of jealousy. For one, she had no claim on him and for another, he had probably known "Jen" since they'd been in diapers. "Yes, and she sent along some things for Mrs. P. With instructions to get sausage."

Brody did smile then. "Mrs. P.'s favorite. I should have thought of it."

But you have enough on your mind, don't you. The thought rushed to the surface of her mind but she kept it there. She'd save it for another time. When they were alone at the ranch and could talk without half the town sending curious glances their way as they were doing now.

"She also mentioned a dance. You know anything about that?"

The lines dissipated slightly, replaced by a warmth she suddenly realized she'd missed over the past few tense days. "Yeah. Annual barbecue out at Prairie Rose. Steak and pie and the Christensen brothers come out and play for a barn dance." He eyed her curiously. "You should stay. Unless you need to get back to Marazur. It's always a good time, and..."

"And what, Brody?" Her heart leaped at what he might say next.

"And if Mrs. P. is still under the weather, she could probably use a second set of hands."

Of course. Her excitement deflated, taking any shred of hope she might have had with it. Of course it was about Mrs. Polcyk and not about dancing with her at all. It all made perfect, depressing sense.

She forced a bright smile. "Speaking of Mrs. P., she did send a list." Lucy tried to adjust the bags to get out the sheet of paper.

"Here," Brody said, taking them from her hands. "Let's put these in the truck first."

He carried her bags to the truck and returned, gesturing to the entrance. "Let's go pick up what we need and head back."

Lucy had never been to anything like it, and she shook off her doldrums. There were stalls of home-grown vegetables, a fruit vendor from British Columbia with glorious peaches and apples, cherries and apricots. Another of baked goods and a huge tent filled with herbs and vegetables from a Hutterite colony. She picked up a bunch of dill and remembered her mother's cucumber salad. There were crafts and the sausage maker and a flower stall.

At the end of it their arms were full. Wordlessly they went back to the truck and headed out of town, back toward Prairie Rose.

Lucy looked over at Brody, unable to forget what she'd learned—and what she hadn't—this morning. Maybe talking to him would help.

"How was your morning?"

"It was fine." He stared straight ahead. The radio played in the background, and she wanted to reach over and turn it down, but figured it would only make him more wary.

"Where did you go?" she tried again, even though she had a suspicion about where he'd been anyway.

"Just around."

"Brody, why don't we try something new. Why don't you just come out with the truth and we'll take it from there."

She was aware how much of a hypocrite she was being. If he'd asked her the same probing questions, she would have evaded them, too. But she *had* told him some of her past. Certainly more than he'd shared with her, and it was clearly wearing on him. What Agnes had revealed this morning only made her more curious. More concerned. If it was causing him this much stress, maybe she could help. He'd gone through most of it alone. And if she were any judge, he'd have refused any sympathy or coddling.

"Right. Like what?"

She smiled faintly. The wife they'd save for another time. "We could start by you admitting you were visiting your father today."

She hadn't known his face could be so hard.

"Who told you that?"

"No one. I mean, I did hear that your dad was in a nursing home, and I put two and two…"

"Well you can stop it."

"Why?" She pressed on, wondering why after all this time it should bother him so much.

"Lucy…"

"Are you still angry with him?"

Brody braked and pulled the truck over along the shoulder of the road. He shoved it in Park and half turned to face her.

"Angry? Why the hell would I be angry?"

The words slashed through the cab of the truck. "You tell me," she bit back. They both knew he *was* angry, whether he should be or not.

After a few interminable seconds, Lucy said more quietly, "It's okay, you know. I understand being angry. I'm really angry with my mum right now. And angry at myself for being angry. Pretty screwed up, huh."

Brody stared at her.

"Yes," he said finally, and the word sounded exhausted. "Yes, I'm angry. I'm angry that he left Prairie Rose vulnerable, and I'm angry he took matters into his own hands, and I'm angry how much it cost me to have to clean up the mess myself."

Without another word, he put the truck back in gear and they drove to the ranch in utter silence.

Chapter Eight

Brody shut the door to the truck and exhaled for the few seconds it took for Lucy to get out. He should have known taking her to town would be a mistake. He should have foreseen that anyone she met would wag their tongue. But he'd been deliberately insulting the other day and he didn't like the cool way she'd treated him since, so he'd thought getting away might thaw the ice a little. Might make up for the way he'd treated her and make it easier for them to work together. The polite silence that marked their relationship lately felt awkward.

He realized Lucy wasn't like Lisa, and the

longer he spent time with her the more sure of it he became. He'd taken her to the soddy to test her, to confirm his suspicions that she considered herself above a hovel of dirt. Instead she'd felt the same way about it that he used to feel. She was continually surprising him, and it threw him off.

"I'll just take these things in," he heard her say, and turned his head. She was standing at the back of the truck with the bags in her hands. A tiny puff of wind ruffled her curls and sent one fluttering against her cheek. But there were no more questions. For once what he'd said had shut her up completely. If he didn't know better, he'd think he'd hurt her feelings. But that was silly, wasn't it?

"You got your ears filled in town, I expect."

She shifted her weight. "Maybe a little."

"And you're curious now. I should have known better than to take you with me."

She put the bags on the ground and stepped forward. "And you don't want me asking any more questions, do you, Brody."

"No."

He looked past her shoulder, not wanting to look into her knowing eyes and see pity there. Someone had told her about his father but she didn't know the half of it. He couldn't stand the thought of how she'd look at him if she knew all the details.

The morning had been hard enough. His dad had been having one of his bad days. Brody's fingers clenched. Seven years. Seven years and the weight of it still lay heavily upon him.

He remembered Lucy's dancing eyes as she'd looked over her shoulder at the soddy. Would she think less of him, of Prairie Rose, if she knew what had happened all those years ago?

His eyes dropped to her lips. Kissing her at the soddy had been a mistake. He'd known it from the moment he'd put his mouth on hers. And what was worse, he wanted to do it again. Badly.

Maybe it *would* be good to trust someone, to have her understand. "But maybe I should answer them, anyway," he said softly. "When you're done unpacking, come out for a ride with me," he suggested. His fingers itched to touch her hair. The fresh floral scent of it reached him on the breeze. Maybe being with her was what he needed; to take his mind off everything his father had said…and hadn't said…this morning.

Something flickered in the depths of her eyes. A little bit of fear, and maybe a little bit of resentment. He couldn't really blame her after the way he'd treated her. He smiled then, knowing exactly how to bribe her. "I'll let you ride Ahab."

Her nose crinkled a little, scrunching up her freckles as the smile dawned on her face. He didn't know how he'd missed that before. It made him want to kiss that particular spot.

But she stepped back, walking backward along the side of the truck until she reached the tailgate, the impish grin still lighting her face.

"You'll let me ride your prized stallion." she asked, tilting her head to one side. "You'll *trust* me."

"If you don't want to..." He nearly laughed at the look on her face. He needed to get away, just for a little while. And he wanted to do it with her.

"That's an offer I can't refuse," she replied, picking up her bags. "Give me ten minutes."

Lucy put the groceries away and dashed upstairs for a hat. She dug into her bag, pulling out a straw cowboy hat and punching it back into its proper shape. She wore ball caps most days to keep her hair tamed and the sun from her eyes. In Marazur she'd gotten a few wry smiles when she'd gone to the barns in her cowboy hat. But it was a part of who she was. And today it would keep the sun off the back of her neck.

She quickly changed into proper boots at the door. She couldn't deny that she was excited about riding Ahab. It meant Brody was beginning to trust her. After his outburst in the truck, she'd nearly despaired of getting answers, and had known she couldn't pry them out of him. But something had changed. Something between them, and as she strode to the stables in the blinding sun, she made herself forget about going to Marazur or brokering deals.

It was Brody she wanted.

He was waiting, standing at the gap of the sliding doors, a set of reins in each hand while the horses stood quietly behind him. Waiting for her, and she wondered briefly what it would be like to have it this way all the time.

"You were fast."

His deep voice echoed and her pulse fluttered. "Opportunity knocked," she replied, a little breathlessly. She pulled a pair of gloves out of her back pocket and slid them on.

When he handed her the reins, their fingers touched, burning through the leather.

They mounted up. Brody adjusted his hat and dashed her a wicked grin. "You won't have trouble keeping up today," he grinned. And he set off at a trot, this time heading dead west.

They rode that way for a long time, not speaking, yet somehow connected. When he'd snapped at her in the truck, she had figured she would never know what had happened at Prairie Rose, or about his wife. But Brody verbalizing his anger had somehow opened a door, one where he was offering to let her in. She'd meant what she said about helping him. Understanding him.

They reached a promontory and Brody stopped. There was a large boulder to one side, but nothing else besides waving prairie grass. Straight ahead lay the jagged line of the Rockies. They were devoid of snow now in August, but somehow their sharp peaks were softened by a hazy summer glow. She slid out of the saddle and merely dropped the reins…it would be enough for Ahab to stay where he was.

"Wade's Butte," she murmured, turning in a circle.

"You knew."

He'd dismounted and come to stand beside her.

"Mrs. P. mentioned it when I first arrived. Said something about getting you to bring me here before I left. I thought maybe we were going there the other day, but you showed me the soddy instead."

She turned a quarter turn and looked at him. It was hard to believe anything could get to him. There wasn't a weak spot to be seen. His dark T-shirt showed where muscles dipped and curved through his arms, back and chest, his trim hips and long legs were steady and sure. His jaw was strong, unrelenting. He was, in a word, splendid.

"What?"

His lips formed the single word as he stared out toward the mountains.

"I was just thinking how appearances can be deceiving."

"Oh?"

She nodded. "Looking at you, Brody Hamilton, no one would guess you were hiding a broken heart." His head snapped sharply, his gaze clashing suddenly with hers as he opened his mouth to deny it. "Unless," she continued quickly, "they had also had their heart broken."

"I don't do broken hearts," he insisted, looking away again.

"Oh, I think you do," she said softly. "And I think your father is the least of it."

Brody sighed heavily. "Let me turn the boys out, and we'll sit down."

He slid the bridles off the horses, letting them graze on the fresh grass free of the bits in their mouths. Lucy perched on the boulder, the surface cool through her jeans even through the glare from the sun. "Wade's Butte was named after my grandfather," he said, coming to sit beside her. "He used to come here a lot. He used to take a few days every fall, come out, pitch a tent and go hunting."

Lucy craned her neck around, searching the grass for evidence that didn't exist. "He did?"

"He was a real man of the land, Granddad. My grandma…" He paused and swallowed. "My grandma used to come along sometimes. They'd build a fire and…"

Again he broke off. Lucy lifted her knees and folded her arms around them.

Brody leaned forward, the gleam in his

eyes intense. Lucy's hands came away from her knees. Her voice was a husky whisper. "They'd build a fire and…"

"You can guess," he answered, his voice a sexy rumble that came from the center of his chest. His fingers plucked her hat from her head, dropping it to the dry grass. As his hands sank into her hair, her heart trembled. She could well imagine what his grandparents had done around a blazing campfire with the wide-open prairie spread out beneath them. Had he brought his wife here, too? The thought slid away into oblivion as his dark gaze centered on her lips, clung there.

She took off his hat, too, dropping it beside hers and running her fingers through the short black strands of his hair. His eyes closed briefly, and when they opened they stared right into her core. There was no point in denying the attraction now or making excuses. It was all too clear to both of them; it was bigger than any of the secrets they'd been hiding.

They both leaned forward, meeting in the middle. His mouth met hers hungrily, his hands moved to link his fingers with hers, and she felt the connection to her toes. She heard a moan and realized it was her own as he released one of her hands to reach around her back, cradling her ribs.

The shift in weight pushed her back until she was lying on the flat surface of the boulder. "Luce," he whispered, looking down at her as his weight pressed her into a natural cradle in the stone.

"This is why you brought me here," she said, looking up at him, wishing he didn't thrill her so, but unable to deny it. His using the shortened version of her name drew them even closer together. She knew that any time someone called her that ever again, she'd think of him. And remember. Remember this moment, of feeling strong and protected and *wanted*.

"Yes," he replied, the word a dark confirmation as he lowered his head again and her lashes fluttered shut.

For long minutes they kissed, hands exploring over cotton clothing, taking their time.

Her fingers grabbed on to his T-shirt, crumpling the jersey as his tongue swept down the curve of her neck. Images of making love to him here under the sun surged through her brain, making her blood race hot. His hand slipped beneath her shirt and pushed it up, revealing the hollow of her belly, and he slid down, his mouth leaving a hot trail from the neck of her T-shirt down her cotton-covered breasts to the skin along the ribs, making her shudder with want. He kissed the soft skin there, then dipped his tongue in her navel and she gasped, arching her back as desire made her limbs heavy.

And she knew what it was to lose all sense. The sun seeped through her eyelids and she lifted her hands to cradle his head. Somewhere in the back of her mind she knew she should stop this and get him to talk, as she'd intended. But being in his arms felt too good; too right.

He had to stop, before they couldn't. Sex would be a mistake, one she couldn't take back.

She froze, and thankfully Brody seemed to understand. He paused, braced up on his hands above her. Letting out a breath, he pressed his forehead to hers. "I'm sorry," he murmured.

Her pulse leaped again. "You don't have anything to be sorry for." If anyone did, it was her. His conscience was clean. He wasn't the one lying about who he was.

He pushed up and away and she felt momentarily naked, which was silly since she was still fully clothed. There was something seductive about being sprawled on a rock in the middle of nowhere. She found she couldn't be sorry they'd done it. But neither would she make the mistake of letting it go further.

She brushed her hair out of her eyes and sent him a flirty smile. "Thank God for glacial deposits, huh."

The corners of his eyes crinkled.

She smiled up at him, but felt it waver. She was starting to care for him, too much. "You brought me here, knowing this was going to happen, didn't you."

He didn't answer. Perhaps a fling wasn't that big a deal for him. She didn't know him well enough to know for sure. But she wouldn't have guessed it. And she didn't do flings. Under any circumstances.

"Brody? Did you bring me here to have sex with me? Did you think I would?"

He hopped off the rock and grabbed his hat. Had he thought that? It shamed him to think perhaps he had. He'd needed her. Needed to feel close to someone again.

He hadn't really considered making love to her, and when she'd frozen in his arms, he'd backed away. It wasn't fair what he was doing and he knew it. And yet…he'd wanted to be with her.

She straightened her clothing and he couldn't help but feel a bit sorry.

"Maybe we should stick to nice, safe topics," she suggested dryly. "Like your family."

He snorted. "I'm not sure I'd call that a safe topic."

"How did your dad end up in a nursing home?" She asked it quietly, as if she would respect whatever his answer was.

Something about her made him want to just say it and get it over with. She knew less about him than anyone he knew, but somehow she *got* him. He wanted to trust her.

He plucked a blossom from a bush creeping up against the rock, twirling it in his fingers. He'd rather she hear it from him than someone else, and the longer she stayed, the more likely it was that someone would say something. Perhaps it was time.

He cleared his throat, wondering how to begin. "There was a car accident. My mum and Hal—Mrs. P.'s husband—were killed. My dad wasn't. Sometimes—" he lifted his chin, stretching out his neck "—I wish he had. It would have been easier than seeing him this way."

"I'm very sorry." He sat back on the rock, and she reached over, putting a hand on his thigh. The denim was firm and warm. "That must have been very hard on you."

He didn't move, didn't put a hand over hers or turn his head to look at her. "You're here from Navarro stables, and you want—or rather King Alexander wants—to establish some sort of relationship between our two operations. I don't think you understand exactly what that means for Prairie Rose, Lucy. It's not a deal I wanted to jeopardize. But I've done that already. I kissed you when I shouldn't have. I brought you here…" He looked away. Never had he used seduction to get his own way. "This isn't how I normally do things."

"That has nothing to do with the relationship between Navarro and Prairie Rose."

"Thank you for that."

Her dark eyes met his once more. "Please, don't ask me to regret it."

His body surged at her words. He'd expected her to be offended, angry. And instead…his gaze dropped to her full lips. With very little persuasion he'd have her flattened on the rock again. He swallowed. And it still wouldn't be any more right.

She breathed in the sweet air. "I think I understand exactly why this particular place could be special to someone. The prairie's spread out like a giant floor, isn't it. You can see for miles in all directions." She tucked a curl behind her ear. "It's a beautiful paradox…how something so vastly empty can fill a soul so fully."

"I've never heard someone explain it in quite that way before." Indeed, it was as if she'd read his mind. Yet another thing that tethered them together. Lisa had never understood it, not like this.

"You came here a lot, didn't you. After it happened."

"Yeah. Yeah, I did. To clear my mind. Decide what to do next."

Lucy sighed and leaned over, resting her head against Brody's shoulder. He tried to ignore how natural the gesture felt. "It's terrible," she continued, "like living without the compass you've used your entire life. Everything you knew—suddenly it's all gone, and you don't know which direction to turn, and there's no one to tell you what to do or to look to for guidance."

"Like when you lost your mother."

"Yes, like that."

She understood. And knowing it, feeling that connection, made him feel for the first time like talking about it.

"Do you have a Wade's Butte, Lucy?" He turned his head and tilted it down, so that his lips were nearly against her hair.

For the first time in months, Lucy didn't feel alone. She closed her eyes, soaking in the feeling of his hard, solid body up next to hers.

"Sometimes I go for a ride in the mornings. If I manage to wake up early, I take out my favorite mare and watch the sunrise from the cliffs. It comes up over the ocean, everything pink and purple and blue and green. Somehow it keeps me from feeling completely disconnected."

For several minutes they simply sat, shoulder to shoulder.

"How bad *is* your father, Brody? What happened?"

Brody shifted, sliding back on the rock and making space for her in the lee of his legs. She leaned back, every bit of stress that had been lurking in her body shimmering away on the wind as his arm came around her, holding her in place. He held out the pink blossom and she took it in her fingers, admiring the fragile petals. They'd gone to the two extremes, on one side arguing bitterly and at the other, kissing. Now it was as though everything was in balance.

"He's paralyzed from the waist down," Brody murmured in her ear. "But he had head injuries, too. Some days are better than others. And my mother and Hal—" he shook his head slightly "—they were just gone. It didn't make any sense. After it happened, it was Mrs. P. who kept things together. She'd just lost her husband, and yet she stepped in until I could take over. I owed her. Prairie Rose owed her. And the first thing I did was tell her that as long as she wanted it, there was a place for her here. She's stayed ever since."

"Why did Prairie Rose owe her?"

He paused. "You might as well know all of it, I guess. Dad owned Prairie Rose, but Hal had a stake in a new venture… Dad wanted to expand. They'd also taken on a third investor…only it became clear that he wasn't as trustworthy as they thought." Brody's muscles stiffened as he remembered. "He'd been a little too generous with himself. Once the paperwork had been signed, he'd been able to play with the books. Dad found out and he and Hal were determined to look after it themselves. They were all going up to Calgary for the weekend. Mum and Mrs. P. to do some holiday shopping. Dad and Hal to set things straight with the partner. Only, they never made it. They were broadsided, and Mrs. P. was the only one to come out of it with minor injuries. Mum and Hal were on the passenger side where they got hit."

The ramifications hit her squarely. This then, explained not only when Brody had taken over, and his signature on all the paperwork, but also the gap in the files. He'd lost his mother and essentially his father, he'd inherited a ranch, a widow and a set of legal problems she could only imagine were a complete nightmare.

She twisted out of his arms and turned, staring up at him with her mouth open in shock. "How much? How much did he take? That's what happened, isn't it? He embezzled."

"Too much," Brody admitted.

"Tell me you got him."

Brody smiled thinly. "Eventually. I hadn't known anything about it. But I didn't try to do like Dad. I didn't go after him myself. I let the RCMP do that. We didn't get any money back, though."

Lucy lifted her hand and touched her fingers to his cheek. There was a rough layer of stubble along his jaw. She imagined what it must have been like to be as young as he was and to lose everything. And to have that much responsibility placed squarely on his shoulders. Her mother had asked that she go to Marazur with Alexander. To give him a chance. That was nothing, nothing compared to what Brody had faced.

He pulled away from her touch, and a muscle ticked in his jaw. "And this is why I didn't want to tell you. Because of the way you're looking at me right now. I never wanted you to feel sorry for me."

But Lucy didn't back away. "Of course not. You're too busy being responsible for everyone. You don't have time for pity."

His black eyes bored into her for long seconds. He hadn't expected her to understand, she could tell. But she did. She understood more about Brody than he realized.

"I *am* responsible. I had a responsibility to Mrs. P. To Hal and Dad. To my mum. To Prairie Rose."

"No one can possibly expect themselves

to carry all that alone." No mention of the nameless wife. Where had she been through all of this? When had she abandoned him? And why?

"There was no one else. My father—" For the first time his voice broke and Lucy knew just how much strain he'd been under. "My father wanted Prairie Rose to be the best. He'd wanted to move forward with a new breeding program and build a reputation for us. He did, but not in the way he wanted. It was up to me to do that for him."

"And so an arrangement with Navarro accomplishes that."

"Yes, it does. And it's why I didn't tell you this before. I didn't want to ruin it."

The noon sun deepened, losing its sharp glare and mellowing over them. A hawk circled overhead, soaring higher and higher. Lucy followed it with her eyes for a few moments.

He needed Navarro. And she needed Prairie Rose.

"It occurs to me, Brody, that we've been fighting each other when it would have been better to work together. Only…"

"I didn't trust you."

She realized she was still partially within

the circle of his arms. A few inches forward and she could be in his embrace again if she wished. This explained so much. And it only served to make her want him more.

"But you trust me now."

"For some reason that escapes me." For the first time he pressed his lips together in a small smile. She answered with a smile of her own, which grew and widened until they were both grinning at each other.

"Well I'll be damned," he muttered, and she thrilled to see his eyes twinkle at her.

"What?"

"I didn't want to tell you. I thought you'd see it as a reflection on the ranch. But you don't, do you?"

"Of course not. It was hardly your fault. I told you before. I judge by what I see."

"Thank you." The words were simple, but Lucy heard the heartfelt meaning behind them. It was like one of the barriers between them had crumbled away.

"Let's work together, then. You need me to establish a relationship with His Highness. And I need you to prove that I'm capable of this job."

"Oh, I bet King Alexander already knows you're capable."

She was unable to stop the glow that spread through her at his easy praise. "I wouldn't be so sure." Only she knew the conversation she'd overheard between Alexander and her half brother the night before she'd departed. "I'm new, I'm young, I'm a woman in a male-dominated industry. And I'm also sure that we can come to an arrangement that will benefit both of us."

"I thought if you knew, you'd take your business elsewhere."

And if you knew who I really am, all bets would be off.

She dropped her eyes, staring at the flower in her fingers. The ranch had been aptly named. Prairie Rose. Beautiful. Strong. And resilient.

He trusted her. She pushed away the stab of guilt. She wished she could trust him, too. And she knew she could, about some things. But how could she possibly tell him now? Tell him who she was. If today had shown her anything, it was that Brody was a man of integrity. He'd definitely think twice about signing with someone who'd misrepresented themselves. What she'd told him was true, all of it. But she wasn't naive enough to believe that there weren't such things as lies of omission.

If she told him the truth they wouldn't be sitting on a boulder in the summer sun. And she wanted that desperately. Men like him didn't come along every day. And all too soon she'd be gone. Did she really want to waste what little time they had? Or could she keep quiet and work with him without the resistance that had plagued them thus far? She'd go back to Marazur with an agreement to prove her competence to her father, and Prairie Rose would have the prestige of a professional relationship with the King of Marazur.

"Lucy?"

She forced herself to look up and tried desperately to ignore the guilt of perpetuating her own deception. Maybe if she'd said something earlier...but now it was too late.

"I'm sorry," she whispered, wondering if those two words could possibly cover everything she was feeling.

"Come here," he commanded, opening his arms. She went into them willingly, the need for him overriding everything. She pulled her knees up to her chest and let him cradle her in his arms, her forehead against his neck so that his pulse beat reassuringly against her skin. The horses grazed, unconcerned at the turn of the afternoon, their hides gleaming as their tails swished the flies away.

And being held in his arms, Lucy realized the one truth she'd never expected: she'd been waiting for Brody all her life. Someone strong and secure and reliable. Someone who could face life's challenges and come out stronger and better. She'd never had that. Not in the whole time growing up. Alexander and her mother had made sure of that.

She pushed back, tilting up her head. The last time he'd kissed her. This time she wouldn't wait.

She touched her mouth to his, felt his breath mingle with hers as they hovered there. His lashes settled on his cheeks and she had the absurd urge to kiss his eyelids.

His teeth caught her lower lip before he pulled away.

"This probably shouldn't happen again. It makes things complicated."

"No, of course not. Neither one of us needs complications." She knew it was right despite the disappointment that settled heavily in her chest.

He thinned his lips and let out a whistle, calling the horses, and tucked his shirt back into his jeans. She slid off the rock and picked up her hat, jamming it on her head.

He put the bridle back on Ahab, slipping the bit into his mouth and giving him a pat before handing the reins to Lucy. But when she grabbed them, he didn't let go.

"I didn't mean for any of that to happen today," he said, and she knew the note of apology in his voice was genuine.

"I know that."

"And it shouldn't happen again. Letting this get too personal…"

"Brody." She knew what he was going to say and wanted him to stop. He couldn't be nice on top of everything. It would only make everything more difficult.

He looked her square in the eyes. "We both know this can't go anywhere. You're going back to Marazur and I'll never leave the ranch. I don't want you to get hurt."

She nodded mutely.

"It's for the best."

He turned to retrieve his mount's bridle, leaving her standing holding Ahab's reins, her eyes wide.

This wasn't in the plan at all.

She'd gone and fallen in love with Brody Hamilton.

Chapter Nine

How it had happened she wasn't sure. It certainly hadn't been part of the plan and it was silly for it to have happened after only a few short weeks. But there it was.

She'd fallen for a man she could never have.

Lucy made her way back from the barns, her heart heavy. She'd thought her life in Marazur had been complicated. Not wanting to fit in but trying anyway, resenting her father yet trying to please him at the same time. Feeling shut up in the palace and yet having the freedom she'd been given at the

stables. All of it was extremely uncomplicated next to her feelings for Brody.

And he'd done nothing but revert back to
his cold, businesslike self since the afternoon
at Wade's Butte. For days she'd wanted to ask
about his ex-wife but couldn't find a way to
without prying. He had a right to his own
secret, even if not knowing was driving her
crazy.

She shut the screen door quietly behind
her. Tomorrow Prairie Rose was holding the
annual barbecue and barn dance; the one Jen
at the bakery had mentioned. And Lucy was
seriously considering finishing up her business at Prairie Rose and leaving in the morning, before the festivities.

She entered the kitchen and found Mrs.
Polcyk wrist-deep in pie crust and the un-
conventional sight of Brody peeling apples.
She watched his strong wrist rotate the fruit
as his paring knife cut thin curls of peel, the
coils dropping onto a newspaper.

His smile stopped her in her tracks. It was
more open than she'd ever seen it, teasing
and warm. "You didn't think I knew how to
peel an apple?"

Her lips quivered as Mrs. P. worked the

pastry. "I didn't expect to find you here, that's all."

"Tomorrow's a big day. I've got the boys getting the loft ready for the dance and setting up the stage for the band. But before that, there's food."

"The boys? Those men are old enough to be your father."

Mrs. P. interjected dryly. "Yes, but aren't all men really boys, Lucy?"

She giggled as Brody's hip shot out and gave the housekeeper a definite nudge, making her adjust her balance.

Then Mrs. P. turned her head, her hands still in the mixing bowl, and sneezed into her own shoulder. "You're still fighting that cold," Lucy observed. "You're sure it's not hay fever or ragweed or something?"

Mrs. P. shrugged. "I've been taking over-the-counter stuff all week. It'll pass."

But Lucy saw her eyes looked red rimmed.

"I was thinking…you've been so great to me, but I don't need to contribute to the workload any more than I already have." It sounded logical to her ears. "I thought I'd leave in the morning and drive to Calgary, and take a flight out later in the day."

"Before the dance?"

She nodded. She could feel Brody's eyes on her but didn't want to look at him. Everything had changed for her since the trip to town and the afternoon at the butte. What she wanted from him and what was to be were two very different things. It would hurt less just to make a clean break. Brody didn't love her. And even if he did…the situation was impossible.

"You should stay. It's a fun day. You'd get to meet other ranchers, neighbors…"

But Mrs. P. broke off, tucking her head against her shoulder again. She slapped the ball of dough into the bowl and went to the sink to wash her hands. "I'm going to take something," she grumbled, and left the kitchen.

Brody calmly sliced apples into a bowl. "So you want to leave."

"I think that's best." When he didn't look up, she continued softly, "Don't you?"

Plop, plop. Slice after slice hit the bowl. He threw away one core and picked up another peeled apple. "You mean after the other day."

She swallowed. How could they talk about what had happened? To verbalize what they'd done…what she'd felt lying there in his arms…was impossible.

"Yes, after the other day. Nothing can happen, right? I mean I have to leave eventually. A day or two early shouldn't be a big deal."

"Mrs. P. was right about tomorrow. It's a lot of fun, and a chance for you to experience real western hospitality. Steaks on the grill and a night of dancing. Our way of celebrating the end of summer."

A night of dancing. She could imagine dancing with Brody, being held in his strong arms. It would be sweet. Bittersweet, knowing she was leaving. Why torture herself when she didn't need to? Being with Brody was a beautiful dream, not reality. And she'd learned not to indulge in dreams. It wasn't worth the thud at the end.

"You don't want me here, Brody." She paused. "You never have."

He finally looked up from his apples and their gazes caught. He looked on the verge of saying something for several seconds, then his shoulders relaxed as he changed his mind. He tossed away another core and picked up another apple. "If nothing else, think of Mrs. Polcyk. There's a lot for her to do, and she could use your help. I've never seen her under the weather for so long before."

Lucy stepped forward, concerned. "Do you think she might be ill?"

"I don't think so. But perhaps run down a bit. When she got sick I suggested postponing tomorrow but she insisted."

"Which is why you're paring apples."

He looked up again, his smile small and lopsided. "Exactly."

The knife grew still in his hand. "Stay," he said softly, and her heart turned over. If he only knew how much she wanted to do just that. "Stay and go back on Monday as you planned."

When he spoke to her that way she wasn't sure she could deny him anything.

"All right, then. I'll look after what I need to and ask Mrs. P. what I can do to help."

"Thank you, Lucy," he replied.

She got the sinking feeling she was making a mistake. But she'd agreed and now she had to send all the information to her father by email rather than in person. He'd been already waiting to hear what she'd negotiated and his last message had sounded a little impatient.

"Tell Mrs. P. I'll be back down later to help," she murmured. "Excuse me."

The upstairs was quiet. It was just as well, anyway.

Lucy was going to go over her notes one last time and then type an email to her father to finalize arrangements. Then she'd be able to focus on helping Mrs. P. and enjoying herself at the dance. Once that was over, she'd have to pack for her departure.

For leave she must, and they both knew it.

She opened her closet to get out her laptop and spied the skirt and blouse she'd bought from Agnes.

Straightening, she ran a finger over the soft floral print and beneath the satin fringe. She knew tomorrow was just a barbecue and as suited to jeans and boots as not, but she wanted to wear it. Wanted Brody to see her in something other than faded denims and her customary T-shirts. She wanted…she smoothed a hand over her wild curls. She wanted to feel pretty. Like a woman. The way she'd felt lying beneath him at Wade's Butte.

She shut the closet door with a firm snap, closing the outfit away. Nothing was going to happen between them again. She knew it was the right thing even as her body tingled, remembering his hands on her. She closed her eyes and opened them again, for when they were closed she could only see how his face had appeared above her in the moments before they'd kissed. Dark and dangerous and oh, so alluring.

No, she had to stay focused on business. Anything else would make leaving on Monday far too difficult. She turned to find Brody standing in the doorway to her room.

She shouldn't be glad to see him, but her heart thumped out a welcome anyway.

"Busy?"

She wished he didn't look so good. Seeing him there on the heels of her thoughts doubled the effect. Somehow his tall, dark looks had become her ideal. She shouldered the laptop and tried to smile.

"About to use your internet connection, if I may," she answered.

He leaned lazily against the door frame, his face partially shadowed by the brim of his hat. A frisson of irritation flickered through her. He always wore it, and it lent him a sense of mystery she reacted to whether she wanted to or not.

"You're a little out of sorts, princess," he

commented glibly, but never moved from the door, blocking her exit. She huffed out a sigh of exasperation.

"I wanted to email King Alexander the latest news quickly. Before he's gone for the day." At his continued use of her nickname her temper flared. "Because of the time difference," she snapped. "You're obviously finished with your pie making."

"Tsk, tsk," he teased, leaning back even further. "No need to bite my head off. You know you're welcome to use the office anytime. I've told Mrs. P. that you'll be along shortly to give her a hand. But perhaps you should wait until you're not so hot under the collar."

He couldn't possibly know how much his words hurt, scoring her heart. Perhaps he was teasing, but he was right, she'd been sharp with him when he hadn't really done anything to warrant it. He couldn't know how much she felt as though she could belong here. Except, to do that she'd have to belong to him, and that wouldn't happen.

To compound her humiliation, tears clogged her throat.

She coughed to clear them. She'd never

been a waterworks and she'd done enough crying since arriving at Prairie Rose.

"Hey." Brody pushed away from the wall, and the teasing curve left his lips. "I didn't mean to upset you. I was only kidding. What's wrong?"

Lucy bit down on her lip. There was no way she could tell him she was upset at having to leave. They'd shared some kisses and Brody had proven himself to be strong, resourceful, responsible. But…it wasn't as if he didn't still have secrets of his own. And for him to reveal what he had and omit his ex-wife…that told her exactly how deep the hurt went. She couldn't compete with that. Staying for the weekend was just prolonging the inevitable.

"I'm just tired, and anxious to get home again. Living out of a suitcase isn't my thing."

His words came out with a sardonic twist. "I'm sure you are. And I'm sure when you get there all your needs will be attended to."

"I didn't mean it that way!" The shoulder strap to the case slipped and the laptop thumped to the floor. "There has been nothing lacking in your hospitality." She stared into his cold eyes and couldn't resist adding, "Mrs. Polcyk has seen to that."

His gaze ignited. "Yes, she has. Still, not the equivalent of the House of Navarro, is it."

Her blood fired. "You know it isn't." What was he trying to accomplish? He knew as well as she did that Prairie Rose was lovely but it was no Mediterranean palace. Nor would either one of them have wanted it to be. He was baiting her and she wasn't sure why. If he was trying to push her away he was going the right way about it.

"I bet you live like a real princess, don't you, Lucy!"

She froze. The nickname was one thing but this was a little too close for comfort. She felt the color leach from her face. Two more days. Surely he wouldn't guess the truth so close to her date of departure. Wouldn't that be a kick in the pants.

The only thing she could do was call his bluff, to see if he meant it the way it had sounded. "Naturally. His Highness treats everyone equitably and with the greatest courtesy."

She sensed, rather than saw, his eyebrows lift. She'd heard her own words, haughty and dismissive and for the first time realized she'd *sounded* like a princess. She faltered, embarrassed. But she couldn't let Brody see her weakening. She covered her mistake with an added barb. "King Alexander never resorts to pointless arguments."

"Dammit, Lucy, you go too far!" He took a step into the room and she planted her hands on her hips. The haughtiness fled only to be replaced by temper. Lord, the man knew how to push her buttons!

"What are you going to do, Brody? Kiss me? It occurs to me that you have three gears—argue, kiss or the cold shoulder!"

She paused. She wanted him to kiss her. Her eyes dropped to his lips, knowing how deceptively soft they really were. Remembering how each tiny touch had ignited her skin. She wanted it again so badly that she could already feel his mouth on hers, even though he was glaring at her from four feet away.

She didn't want to argue. She didn't want him to walk away from her. What she wanted was to forget about all the reasons they were apart and simply launch herself into his strong arms. Feel his body against hers, the heat of his mouth on the soft skin beneath her ear.

"And what if I did? What if I kissed you?" His voice became soft, silky.

What he said only fueled her further. Her

tongue slipped out over her lips. She had to stop this now. She was leaving in a few days, and to have anything more between them would be a mistake they would both regret. For him it would be kissing. For her it would be putting feelings into actions, and that was a whole other issue. She couldn't bear for history to repeat itself. Alexander and her mother had set an example she didn't want to follow, and it was impossible to miss the similarities in situation.

"We both agreed that was a bad idea," she stammered, taking a retreating step. She wanted it so badly she ached, but if he kissed her, she'd be lost…and tempted to tell him how she felt.

"You're right. It is a bad idea. And I'm not in the habit of making bad choices."

Oh, that stung.

"So now I'm a bad choice," she defended tartly, lifting her chin. He was giving her what she wanted…an escape route, and all she could do was to be angry with him for it. The man was so exasperating! Just when she'd decided to keep things as calm as possible before she departed, he had to come in here and push all her buttons, good and bad.

"Absolutely."

Her nostrils flared. "Worse than *she* was?"

The words flew out before she could think, and her lips sealed shut again as Brody took another menacing step.

"Her who?" he asked, the question low with warning, but she couldn't turn back now. It might be her only chance to know.

"You know who," she whispered. It was difficult to hold his gaze but she knew she must. "Your ex-wife."

He looked away first, staring out her window even though she knew he couldn't see anything at this distance.

She hadn't meant to blurt it out. He was entitled to his own secret. Now she'd gone and revealed that she'd known about his previous marriage.

She'd felt that same panic of discovery only moments ago when he'd made the princess comment. And now she was unfairly turning it on him. The obstinate set of his jaw told her he was loath to discuss it. And the way he avoided her gaze told her how much it still hurt him.

"Damn Mrs. Polcyk." The words were quiet and bitter.

"It wasn't her. She didn't betray your confidence. I'm sorry, Brody. I shouldn't have mentioned it. It was low. You provoked me and I blurted it out."

His head turned slowly toward her. "Taking you to town was a bigger mistake than I realized."

He was making this more awkward with every word.

"I didn't go prying, I promise. There was a picture of your family at the antique shop…"

"Agnes. And you didn't say anything."

"It wasn't my place, Brody. You have a right to your own secrets." Even though it hurt her to know it.

To her surprise he sighed and went to the window. She had expected him to argue and rail, but he didn't. He just treated it with a calm acceptance. Somehow she preferred the argument. It was what she understood. Especially since her own life had been turned upside down.

She waited, biting back the burning questions bubbling within her. The fact was he'd trusted her with the truth about Prairie Rose and his father, but he hadn't trusted her with this. And the past with the ranch was very painful, so that told her very clearly how much his divorce had cost him.

And now she'd fallen for him and wanted

him to trust her with everything, knowing full well she had no right. Not when she was keeping such an important secret from him. "Do you want to talk about it?"

His reply was a dry, sardonic huff. "What do you think?"

Lucy bent and picked up the fallen laptop, putting it on the bed.

"I was right," she said finally, "when I said you had a broken heart. Because if she hadn't hurt you that much you'd be able to look at me right now."

He turned, the jut of his chin angled, trying to prove a point. "Do I strike you as the kind of man who talks his feelings to death?"

Lucy went to him, laid a hand on his arm. "You look like you'd rather be doing anything else."

His eyes fell on the spot where her hand met his arm.

It was pale against his darker skin. "It doesn't matter anymore. It was over a long time ago."

"You don't trust me, and that's okay." Her fingers glided down and linked with his. She got it. She didn't trust him with the truth, either.

"We've only known each other a few weeks."

"I know." She circled her thumb over his fingers. "Crazy, isn't it." Yeah, crazy that she cared about him so much in such a short amount of time.

"And this isn't part of your job."

"As much as we try, this stopped being about the job a long time ago."

"I know."

Brody pulled her into his arms. She felt good there, tucked against his chest, the flowery scent of her hair filling his nostrils. He wanted to trust her but knew why he didn't. And each time he held her, he knew it would be that much harder watching her leave. He argued with her because it was so much easier than admitting his feelings for her were more than they should be. Or could be. Yet she had this crazy way of keeping them together and making him tell her things he normally didn't speak of to anyone. He wasn't sure how she did that.

"Lisa married me expecting one thing and getting another. The ranch was profitable. It was expanding. We were making plans to build a new house for us. Something big, that's what she wanted. To make a statement. I loved her and was too blind to see she wanted that more than she wanted me."

"When?" Lucy asked simply. The warmth of her breath seeped through his shirt, and he closed his eyes.

"A few months after the accident. I was in charge of the ranch, and the money issue had come out."

Lucy pushed away and looked up at him. "You mean the fraud."

"Yes."

"You're kidding. She left you then?"

"She hadn't signed on for that, you see."

Lucy's lips pursed as if she'd just tasted something sour. A bubble of laughter rose in his chest. "For God's sake, Lucy. You don't need to get all indignant on my behalf. It's over and done."

"But that's cruel."

"It was at the time. But at least she was honest about what she wanted in the end. She wanted a life I couldn't give her and had the sense to leave rather than drag things out and make us both unhappy."

Lucy went strangely quiet. She walked over to the bed and sat down. After several moments she looked up again. Her dark eyes were the most serious he'd ever seen them. "Is that why you resent me so much? You think I'm like her? You think the *kind* of life

I have is more important to me than the people in it?" She blinked. "Is that why you call me princess?"

Though it could well be a mistake, he went to the bed and sat down on the spread beside her.

"Yes," he admitted, "but only at first. I don't think you're like Lisa now. I realized that the day I took you to the soddy and you didn't look down your nose at it. But the fact is we *are* from different worlds. And you must go back to yours soon. You wouldn't be happy somewhere like Prairie Rose." He looked away. He couldn't meet her eyes as he delivered one last truth: "I'm not sure I even believe in love, anyway."

He felt her shift beside him but continued on. He was right about this. Prairie Rose couldn't compare with Marazur and he wouldn't have believed her if she'd said it could. She had the job of a lifetime there and all the comforts she could ever want. And he wasn't in love with her. He couldn't be; he hardly knew her.

"Look, Lisa said she loved me but she didn't, not really. I'm not sure I was really in love with her, either."

"You don't mean that."

"I do."

Lucy spun on the bed, tucking one leg beneath her. It was the damnedest thing. She had him talking about things he'd never spoken to anyone about. It wasn't exactly a comfortable feeling, this outpouring of honesty.

"But, Brody…it's not in you to be in anything halfway. You put one hundred percent of yourself into everything you do. If I know anything from my time here it's that you care too much!"

He jumped up, spinning away from her. That was preposterous. This would all be better once she was gone for good. He wouldn't have to worry about a dark set of eyes tempting him to talk about things that couldn't be changed. Momentarily he hated her for it.

"Look," he said, stopping at the door and attempting to make his face as normal as possible. "You only have a few days left and it's pointless to spend them arguing or talking about stuff that doesn't matter." He ignored the wounded look on her face. Monday she'd be gone and over whatever it was that was between them. "Tomorrow is the barbecue and dance. Let's just enjoy it, okay?" He didn't wait for her to agree, but turned away and walked back down the hall. Dammit, he'd come here with the idea of teasing her about the dance and they'd ended up arguing again. There was no *normal* with them. Anytime he attempted it he either ended up fighting with her or, like today, getting in too deep.

The sooner she was gone the better, because each day she spent here was one more where his feelings grew more complicated.

Chapter Ten

Lucy stared at herself in the full-length mirror. She should just take the outfit off and put her jeans back on. Brody had said they should enjoy today, but she hardly felt as if she could. How would it look to him now, for her to get all dressed up? Like she had designs on him?

The trouble was she did. Even though she knew she shouldn't. And her feelings grew stronger each time they were together.

She spun in front of the antique mirror and frowned. The secret of who she really was weighed even heavier these days. Perhaps she should have been honest with him from the beginning. It certainly would have made things less complicated between them. But she'd needed the time to just *be*. And it was too late to go back now.

Lucy sighed, smoothing her hands over the cotton of the skirt. She looked about fifteen years old in the outfit. She'd gathered her hair back from the sides with a clip and the rest of her gingery curls rioted around her shoulders. It made her appear even younger.

It was foolish to dress up for Brody, anyway. Day after tomorrow she'd be catching a flight back to Marazur and leaving Prairie Rose behind her for good. She'd finally sent that email detailing stud fees and arrangements she'd made on Navarro's behalf. All that was left was to pack her things and drive back to Calgary for her flight home.

There was no denying, though, this place got to her. It was simple and uncomplicated, with no expectations. Here she was just Lucy Farnsworth, pain in the neck. She smiled a little to herself. Perhaps that was why she'd been drawn to it from the beginning. Prairie Rose—and Brody for that matter—seemed to take things to a common denominator. Hard work, loyalty and honor. Without the mess of family drama that marked her life in Marazur.

She turned away from the mirror. The outfit had been purchased in a moment of whimsy, and she'd wear it tonight regardless. It fit her, and made her feel like she fit in here, as well. She'd be back to reality soon enough.

A knock sounded on the door frame and she looked over her shoulder, seeing Mrs. P.'s sparkling eyes watching her. "Mrs. Polcyk! I was coming down to help you. After your cold, you shouldn't be doing all this yourself."

The woman had been cooking for the better part of two days, getting ready for the barbecue. Lucy had been so focused on finishing up business with Brody she hadn't had time to help put things together beyond a half hour of wrapping potatoes in foil this morning.

Mrs. Polcyk stepped into the room, much the same as Brody had the previous day. Lucy smiled. Privacy didn't seem to count for much at the ranch, but she didn't resent the intrusion, which was a surprise in itself. It made her feel included.

"You're a dear, and I appreciate the help," Mrs. Polcyk declared, smiling fondly. She stopped and gave Lucy an appraising glance. "Oh, Lucy. You are a picture."

Lucy smiled shyly. "You think so? I bought it at Agnes's."

"It's lovely. But..." She stared at Lucy's toes, bare except for the pale-pink polish on the nails. "You seem to be missing something."

Lucy looked down at her toes. "I know. I have to polish my boots."

She looked back up to find Mrs. P's eyes twinkling at her. The housekeeper was dressed in a pair of neat jeans and a white cotton shirt with *Prairie Rose* and a matching flower emblazoned on the breast. Her graying hair was gathered in its customary bun.

"I do feel somewhat overdressed," Lucy admitted.

"Nonsense. You look dressed for a dance. Stay here. I have an idea." Mrs. P. scuttled out only to return moments later with a shoe box in her hands. She came right into the room, placed the box on the bed, and lifted the cover.

Lucy reached out and put a single finger on the tip of one lovely pump.

"Oh, they're beautiful." Indeed, the fine navy leather was soft and cut in an intricate pattern, making them appear as though they were constructed of lace. One toe had a tiny scuff mark; otherwise they were unblemished.

"They match your skirt. Try them on."

Lucy sat on the edge of the bed and slipped a shoe over her foot. A perfect fit, which was a surprise. She stuck out her toes, admiring the delicate bow adorning the shoe top.

"They fit!" Mrs. Polcyk let out a delighted laugh.

"Mrs. Hamilton would have been so pleased to see them on a girl as lovely as you."

"Mrs. Hamilton?" Lucy drew her foot back, and a crease formed between her brows. She was still surprised at being called lovely.

"Mrs. Wade Hamilton. Brody's grandmother."

Lucy slipped off the shoe. "Oh, I can't, then. These must be—"

They were vintage, same as her outfit. And so perfect. But it wasn't right. It almost felt as if she was insinuating her way into something, and she didn't want that.

"Oh, sometime around the thirties I'd guess."

She put the shoe gently back in the box.

"Then I absolutely musn't. They're antiques, and an heirloom."

"Did Brody tell you the story about Wade and Delilah when you rode out to the butte the other day?"

Lucy hoped she wasn't blushing; her cheeks felt warm and she couldn't meet Mrs. P.'s eyes. They'd talked of his dad, but other conversation had ceased because they'd been busy doing *other things.* "No, but he did mention it was his grandfather's favorite spot."

"It's named after his grandfather, you know. He used to go there hunting and such, and Delilah…oh, what a pistol she was." Mrs. Polcyk smiled in fond remembrance. "And a crack shot. Wade proposed to Delilah on that very spot. And they went back there every year for their anniversary."

"There's so much history here." Lucy looked longingly at the box. Brody had taken her *there?* A place that had so much family importance? What did that mean? Her heart trembled at the knowledge that he'd taken her somewhere so obviously special. Was it possible he wanted more from her? The soddy had been a test. Had that been another one?

Had she passed?

The thought expanded her chest. What

would it be like to be a part of the Hamilton history? To truly belong? But that was absurd. She made herself push the shoes away. "I can't. It would be presumptuous of me."

But Mrs. P. insisted. "Life is meant to be lived, and shoes were made to be danced in. These have sat alone too long. Brody's mum had large feet, and the younger Mrs. Hamilton…" But she didn't finish the sentence.

"Lisa, you mean."

Mrs. Polcyk nodded, taking both shoes out of the box again. "Brody told me you knew."

"What was she like?"

Mrs. P. laughed, but this time it wasn't filled with her usual mirth. She put the shoes firmly in Lucy's hands. "Not worth a single hair on that boy's head, and that's the truth." She rested her hands on her knees. "Waltzed in here with her nose turned up demanding Brody build them their own place."

"So he said."

"She was beautiful, I'll give her that," the older woman conceded. "A little *too* beautiful for here. Certainly wouldn't have worn secondhand shoes." She angled a knowing look at Lucy. "He'd do better with someone more down-to-earth."

Lucy fought back the urge to laugh. It was

as plain as the nose on her face that Mrs. P. meant her, and while there was a certain attraction to thinking she and Brody might suit each other, she also knew it would never be.

She thought of her opulent suite back in Marazur. It was about as far from down-to-earth as it could get. But when she'd moved there, Alexander had insisted that she be afforded the same comforts as her two half brothers. She frowned again, blinked. Maybe her father hadn't been trying to pressure her at all. Perhaps he'd only been trying to show her she belonged as much as Raoul and Diego did.

Mrs. Polcyk patted her leg and stood, her knees creaking. "You just put on your dancing shoes and come down when you're ready. Neighbors will start showing up anytime, and another pair of hands would be right welcome."

When she was gone, Lucy slipped the shoes on and did a few steps beside the bed, stopping at the mirror. She stared at her reflection. Most girls dreamed about being a fairy-tale princess and going to the ball. Tonight she just wanted to be an ordinary girl, doing a two-step. She reached up and took

the clip from her hair, shaking out the curls
the way she knew Brody liked it best.

He was right. Mrs. Polcyk was right. Life
was meant to be lived. She should enjoy what
little time she had left here.

There would be time enough to face reality tomorrow.

The yard was already filling up with half-
ton trucks and cars as people started arriving. All laughing and smiling, dressed mostly
in what Lucy recognized as everyday special: neat jeans, western shirts, polished boots
and, of course, hats. After one look out the
kitchen window, she turned back to Mrs. Polcyk. "What can I do?"

The older woman smiled warmly and held
up a white cobbler apron. "Put this on so you
don't mess that pretty dress. Brody's already
lit the grills. All that's left to do is the coleslaw. If you don't mind grating cabbage."

"Of course not." Lucy moved swiftly, taking the apron and slipping the loop over her
neck, tying the straps behind her back. A
massive cutting board sat on the counter with
halved cabbage heads waiting their turn to be
made into slaw. She picked up the first and

started grating, stopping every few minutes to fill the huge bread bowl at her side.

"Mind your knuckles, now," Mrs. P. cautioned, as Lucy got close to the end of her cabbage head.

Lucy grinned. "You do realize you can buy this already shredded, in lovely convenient bags."

"Wouldn't be any fun in that," Mrs. P. returned, her smile automatic. "Besides, it's not fresh, that stuff."

Lucy picked up another chunk of cabbage while watching Mrs. P. whisking vinegar and mayonnaise in a bowl. "And you make your own dressing?"

"Of course I do."

She was in the middle of telling Lucy her secret recipe when Brody slammed through the door, his hat set farther back on his head than usual and his eyes sparkling.

"Well, well," he said, teasing Lucy openly. "Here's our princess in an apron."

Her smile froze in place. Now that she knew the reason behind the name, it hit the heart of her even harder. She swiped the cabbage down harder than necessary and felt the scrape of a knuckle against the metal holes.

"Ow!" Her hand flew to her mouth as she sucked on the wounded skin.

Brody stepped forward as Mrs. Polcyk said calmly, "I told you to watch your knuckles."

He took her hand in his and turned it over, examining the scratch. "It appears there's going to be a little bit of you in the salad."

"Shut up," she muttered, trying to pull her hand away. But he held firm.

"You're going to need a bandage on that."

"I can get it myself."

And darn it all if he didn't laugh at her, leaning back from the waist and letting out a full-throated hoot. When he looked back at her, his eyes were gleaming. "You, Miss Lucy, look about ten years old when you stick out your lip like that."

She looked up in his mocking face and resisted the urge to stamp her foot. "Go away and quit distracting me. I can't be much help, if all you're going to do is stand here and aggravate me."

He let go of her hand and she exhaled, relieved that he wasn't touching her anymore. Each time he did her pulse leaped.

"Thank goodness it was only your hand, and not your feet," he remarked, winking. "You're going to need them for dancing later."

"Oh, go *on* with you! Don't you have steaks to grill or something?" He'd winked at her, for Pete's sake. An incorrigible flirt.

"Sure do." He grinned at her for another moment before turning on a booted heel and slamming back out the door. When Lucy sighed, Mrs. Polcyk held out a Band-Aid.

"He's an infernal tease, that boy. I'd forgotten how much."

Her words warmed Lucy. Did she bring something out in Brody he'd kept hidden? He'd seemed to loosen up since her arrival, but she'd thought at first that maybe it was just because they'd gotten to know each other better.

And now an offhand comment about his light mood. She'd like to believe she brought out some of his positive traits; he had so much to offer.

She took the bandage and doctored her knuckle. That way of thinking was pointless. She couldn't seem to reconcile the two things she wanted. Being with Brody had opened up a new world for her, one she didn't want to leave. But it had also made her think more about her relationship—or lack of it—with her father, and something inside her also wanted to explore that further. To get to know the man who had fathered her. To give him a chance. It certainly wasn't something she'd expected.

She picked up a carrot and started grating it to add to the slaw. It was Brody and his steadfastness who had made that possible, she realized. He'd made a promise to his father to look after the ranch and Mrs. Polcyk, in the same way that she'd promised her mother she'd go to Marazur and give Alexander a chance.

Hmm.

"If you're done there, I'll put the dressing on and we can start carrying things out."

"Oh, of course!" She shook away her thoughts and passed the bowl.

For several minutes they carried roasters and bowls to a string of folding tables set up as a buffet. Roasters full of foil-wrapped baked potatoes, baskets of fresh buns and butter, bowls of coleslaw and earthenware pots with homemade baked beans all made their way outside. Brody tended steaks on three separate gas barbecues at the end of the procession of tables, his ever-present hat shading his eyes from the sun. She could still feel his gaze on her every time she passed with her hands full. Finally there was nothing left to put out but the paper plates and cutlery. For a moment she allowed herself the fantasy that this was exactly where she was meant to be. As one of the hosts. As part of Prairie Rose and the community.

Brody looked at Mrs. Polcyk and said, "The first round of steak is ready."

Lucy's smile was as wide as his when Mrs. P. pulled out a rusted triangle and rang it several times, calling everyone to eat.

Lucy stayed behind the tables, helping Mrs. Polcyk to make sure everyone had what they needed. Every few seconds Mrs. P. or Brody would introduce her—to the Bancrofts, the Scholtens, a group of teenagers of various parentage who had come separately from their parents and wore trendy jeans and T-shirts rather than their parents' more traditional western wear. The Christensen brothers filed through; they'd provide the music later.

And on it went, men and women and children laughing and filling their plates and grabbing beers and soft drinks from washtubs filled with ice at the end of the tables. When everyone had gone through, the noise was horrendous, even outside: Lucy saw with some amazement that there were prob-

ably close to a hundred people seated at pic-
nic tables all laid out between the house and
the barn. It was loud and raucous, yet with
a harmony to it, and she smiled to herself.
Brody came behind her and put his hand on
her waist.

"Get something to eat…while there's still
something left."

She grinned. "Yes, boss."

He smiled back, his hat touching her curls.
His face was so close to hers that she could
feel the heat of his breath on the side of her
neck. "Well. It only took you a few weeks to
realize that."

"You wish."

The warmth disappeared but his hand remained on her waist as he leaned back at the
waist, laughing. "You're never going to give
in, are you."

It was meant as a joke, but the words
seemed to ricochet around, hitting each of
them with the truth. As much as she might
want to, she knew Brody would never love
her the way she wanted, and to give in to her
own weakness would only hurt her further.
"No, I'm not," she answered quietly, duck-
ing away from his hand and grabbing a plate.

Mrs. Polcyk was filling her plate, and

Lucy sat with her rather than with Brody, who found a place with a young couple and their kids as well as Jen, the woman from the bakery, who looked fresh and cute in a short jean skirt and boots. Lucy's eyes narrowed. She would not be jealous. She would not. It didn't matter to her one bit who Brody sat with. Or who he dated. It was absolutely none of her business.

"You want to tear her eyes out?"

Mrs. Polcyk's bland observation hit her, and she turned away from the sight of Brody laughing at something Jen said. "What?"

"The way you're glaring. If you want to put your mark on him, do it. I don't think he'd put up much of a fight."

"That's ridiculous."

"Is it?"

"I'm leaving day after tomorrow."

"We're all aware of that." Mrs. Polcyk cut into her steak with her plastic knife, slicing easily through the tender beef. "But a blind man could see there's feelings between you."

"Mrs. Polcyk…please." Lucy lowered her voice. "It's impossible. It's just easier this way."

The woman boosted herself up from her seat and gathered up her plate. "Well, hell," she said lightly. "No one said it was going to be easy, did they?"

Lucy tried to finish her meal after that, but she wasn't very hungry anymore. After a few minutes of pushing her potato around her plate, she gave up and put it in one of the trash bins set around the eating area. She went to help slice and serve pies, and thankfully Mrs. Polcyk said nothing more about it. One by one the pie plates were emptied of apple, cherry and lemon meringue. Washtubs were replenished with cans of pop. Laughter echoed through the barnyard and Lucy stood on the outside, with an untasted piece of apple pie on her plate, wondering how on earth she'd come to love this place so much in such a short time.

While Brody hitched up a small wagon and took the children for a quick hayride, all the women pitched in cleaning up; joking and teasing Mrs. P. and making their way through the kitchen as though it was their own. Lucy smiled and answered questions politely when she was asked.

This was what she remembered about Trembling Oak, too. It was a community. Everyone relied on each other. Of course, everyone stuck their noses in everyone else's business too, but that was a price that was paid. It was knowing that when push came to shove, you weren't alone. It all became too much and Lucy fled before anyone could see the strange look on her face or how she felt the need to cry.

She escaped out the back, taking deep breaths to get her emotions under control. The sun began to set, becoming a beautiful bronze ball that painted the sky with pinks and purples as it dipped toward its bed behind the Rockies. The brash light of summer softened, setting everything with a misty haze. The golden and green fields were dotted with gorgeous, gorgeous horses and railroad tracks of fences.

Music started up, the testing strains of guitar and violin finding their pitch before somehow making their way to an agreed key and song. She listened for a few minutes, her foot tapping lightly. She could skip out on the whole thing and be completely miserable. Or she could join in and enjoy herself and hopefully take back to Marazur a beautiful memory of dancing and laughing on a summer's night.

There really was no choice.

She turned the corner of the house and

headed toward the "old" barn, the one that held no livestock now but served as storage below and an abandoned loft overhead. Battered wooden stairs led up to the loft, with several people standing on the platform outside the double doors that were rolled open. She climbed the stairs and ventured a peek inside.

The band was on a raised platform, nearly laughing as they played a tune and people two-stepped in circles around the floor. Boots and jeans paired up with sneakers and shorts as young danced with old. Benches were lined up against the side of the room for those not dancing, but only a handful of people were seated. The music was lively and good; it would be hard to remain still for long.

At the end of the first song, they went immediately into another two-step. Brody appeared at her side. "Care to?"

"Don't you have host duties?"

"Absolutely. As the host it's my job to dance with the prettiest girl in the place."

"Go on."

"Why else did you dress up in that outfit, anyway? It was made for dancing. Or so Agnes has bragged enough times. It is from her shop, right?"

She lifted her chin and looked away. How could he know that? Unless Mrs. Polcyk had loose lips. After her observations at supper, she wouldn't be surprised.

"And besides, you stared at me all through supper."

Her head snapped around. "You're impossible!"

"Maybe, but I'm a helluva good dancer, Miss Farnsworth. And if you don't want to dance, there's lots of ladies here who will."

He held out his hand and lifted an eyebrow, challenging her.

"Fine," she said with a glare. "One dance. It would look funny if I didn't, I suppose."

She took his hand, shocked when he spun her around quite efficiently and settled his hand at her waist. Instantly he guided her into the easy rocking steps of the dance, the entire swirling circle of dancers moving around the floor as if they did it every day of their lives. And damn his hide, if he wasn't right after all. He *was* a sublime dancer. She'd known how to two-step since she was ten, but he made even spinning turns simple as he guided her first one way, then the other, beneath his arm and bringing her effortlessly back in step.

"I told you."

He grinned down at her as the band thumped and twanged their way on, the rough, enthusiastic quality of the music creating an energy that vibrated from the soles of her feet up. "Hmph."

"Miss Lucy, you're adorable when you pout. It makes *all* of your freckles stand out."

That did it. She stomped down hard with her vintage pump on his toe, breaking their rhythm. She attempted to twist out of his arms but his hand gripped her wrist quite efficiently and swirled her back into the dance.

"Good thing for you I'm wearing boots," he remarked. The teasing smile was still in place but something darker glittered in his eyes.

"You've been an arrogant pain in the behind for the better part of two weeks, and tonight you turn into an incorrigible tease. Go turn your charms on someone else who will appreciate them."

"Do you really want me to?"

"Yes, I think I do."

"Okay."

The music ended and he let her go. The air seemed abruptly cool, now that there was space between them, and she tried very hard not to miss his warmth.

"Thanks for the dance, Lucy."

He walked away unconcerned, and when the band started up again, he crossed the floor and led Jen out for a waltz.

Chapter Eleven

She wanted to stay mad, but it was hard when he danced and smiled so effortlessly with everyone. When the Christensen brothers fired up a polka, she couldn't stop the smile at the sight of him stomping around the floor with Mrs. Polcyk in his arms. When the first group was well winded and left the floor, the band immediately went into another polka, and Lucy was grabbed by a neighboring rancher she dimly remembered meeting at supper.

The band announced a break, and it seemed everyone made a beeline for the tubs full of pop and bottled water. Lucy grabbed a water and twisted off the top, scanning the area for Brody. But he was gone.

She saw lights in the barn and wondered if he'd gone to check on the horses that weren't out in the pasture. Suddenly the cool quiet of the barn sounded more appealing than the dance and crush of strangers. For a while she'd forgotten that she didn't truly belong, but seeing the laughing faces reminded her that she was an outsider. She looked at the long structure, suddenly needing the horses. They'd never failed her before.

She made her way across the soft grass, noting that the barn door was open. What she didn't expect was the youth that came barreling out at save-my-neck speed or the sound of sobbing from within.

She peeked around the corner, and immediately saw Brody, his arms around a girl and his face looking incredibly worn as the girl did her best to soak his shirt through with her tears.

"It'll be okay, Suze," she heard him say gently. "He's a good kid. You both are. It just didn't work out."

"But I love him," came the plaintive reply, borne on hiccupy sobs.

"I know."

That was all. No trying to persuade her it didn't matter, no telling her she was too young for such an adult emotion. The girl couldn't be more than seventeen, but Brody simply offered her a shoulder.

Lucy sighed. How she'd wished for someone like Brody when she was growing up. Someone who would simply accept her and be on her side. No matter what. If she thought he'd be this way for her, she'd explain about her father. But he wouldn't understand. And so she would keep her secret to herself.

At her audible sigh, Brody looked up. He tensed, seeing her there, and the girl straightened and turned when she sensed the change in him.

"I'm sorry," Lucy offered, seeing the girl's sudden embarrassment. "I didn't mean to intrude."

"It's okay." The girl stared at her feet, clearly embarrassed at getting caught out.

"Lucy, this is Suzanne." Brody performed the introduction quietly, his hand still secure, comforting on her shoulder. Protecting her.

"Hello, Suzanne," she offered softly. "I'm Lucy."

She was still trying to get past the gentle way he was looking after the teen. It was so much the way a father would, or a big brother. Both things that Lucy had missed out on growing up. Brody would be such a good father...the thought snuck in unbidden and she chased it away.

The music started up behind them; the band's break was over. "Did you come with Matt?" Brody asked Suzanne.

She nodded, tears threatening again at the boy's name.

"But your mum and dad are here and can drive you home," he continued.

Another nod.

Brody sent a pleading look at Lucy, that said he'd suddenly run out of ideas about what he should do. She stepped in, knowing that the only thing worse than breaking up was breaking up in public and having everyone see the evidence of crying. She stepped closer. "Well, Suzanne, you can't go back to the dance like that, can you." She smiled. "Come on up to the house and I'll help you get fixed up."

"You will?"

"Of course I will."

She ignored the gratitude she knew was in Brody's eyes, instead aiming her smile directly at the distraught teen. She couldn't look at Brody with all these feelings bubbling up inside her. His teasing was infuriating, but his caring tonight only showed her what a good man he was beneath the cocky smile or stony reticence. Seeing this side of him made it even more difficult for her to run away from her growing feelings.

"I'll bring her back," she murmured.

"Thank you, Luce."

A shudder went through her as he used the shortened version of her name. She led Suzanne away, happy to retreat into the cool air of the yard as they made their way to the dark farmhouse.

It was half an hour before they returned to the dance, Suzanne wearing a weak smile and a fortifying coat of makeup and Lucy with a sort of breathless anticipation of seeing Brody again. Of maybe dancing with him. The gaiety was in full swing. Moments after arriving in the loft she was snagged for a two-step and a waltz. Her gaze sought Brody out again and again as they both danced with other people. She sat out a line dance, choosing to watch the younger people boot-scoot. But the singer announced the "barn dance," and pairs formed up into two circles; men on the inside and women on the perimeter. Lucy was captured by an older man with a huge grin and a larger belt buckle. As one couple demonstrated the steps to any newcomers, Lucy memorized them in her mind.

The music started and she faltered only once before being passed on to her new partner. After three more she had the steps down pat and relaxed.

Until she got to Brody.

He didn't smile, and neither did she. He took her hand in his, the warmth seeping through the skin, the heat of it heavy, even though he held her fingers lightly. She followed the steps, at each beat wondering how to say what she wanted and knowing she'd sound like a complete idiot if she said exactly what she was thinking.

They were halfway through the sequence and time was growing short when he said over the fiddle and guitar, "Thanks for what you did for Suzy."

"It was nothing." Their heels touched, then their knees while Lucy struggled to say what she felt before he handed her off to a spotty-faced boy behind her. "You were very good with her, Brody."

His gaze caught hers, dark and magnetic, but the steps pulled them apart.

Another half hour passed, the music getting faster and the laughter louder. She was gasping for air and fanning her face after something frenetic called the Butterfly, when the band slowed it down and called Brody to the stage.

"He thought he could avoid us all night, but it's time for Hamilton to favor us with a tune." At Brody's wave-off, the singer leaned into the mike with a lopsided grin. "Too late now, Hamilton. Get your butt up here."

Lucy watched, amazed, as Brody stepped up onto the stage and took the guitar he was offered. He cradled it against him as he perched on a plain wooden stool, and Lucy trembled as their eyes met. His, so very dark, so knowing, slightly shadowed by the black brim of his hat, yet she knew he was looking straight at her. *Inside* her. The way only he could. Just moments ago she'd been in his arms, cheeks flushed with exertion and flirtation as he took her around the floor in the Butterfly. The memory of the heat of his body close to hers was still present.

He sat on the wooden stool, one long denim-clad leg stretched out straight, ending in his boot which braced against the floor.

And looking down for a moment, he started to play.

It wasn't a song she recognized, but the quiet sound of the guitar filled the loft. Every single person there had stopped to listen, to watch, as their neighbor, their friend, picked out a melody.

He lifted his head and looked straight at her as he started to sing.

This can't be happening, she thought, taking a step backward. He had to be too good to be true. There had to be something about him that would send her in the other direction. A cowboy dedicated to his ranch and his livestock and his family, with a ready smile and a willing hand. One who, she understood now, gave everything for his family. One who would rather die than break his code of honor. On top of all that, he could *sing*.

They'd done such a good job of denying that there was anything more than sexual attraction growing between them; or at least pretending to deny it. Even when they'd kissed out at Wade's Butte, they'd both turned away from it in the end, knowing it would be a mistake. But today he'd seemed to shed all his worries, and it made him sexier than ever. She should look away. She shouldn't be standing like an idiot on the wood floor, gazing like some groupie at the sexy cowboy in the dark hat. She should get out of the barn right now. And get far away.

But then, she knew Brody well enough to know that if she did that, he'd come and find her. She tensed as she considered that possibility. What would happen if he found her at the barn…in the house…by the pond?

Was that what she really wanted, then? Did she want him to find her? If he did she knew what would happen. Whatever this was that had been growing between them wouldn't be denied. Not on a night like tonight. Too much had happened and they were both well aware that time was growing short. So what *did* she want from Brody? A quick roll in the hay? Because anything more from him was out of the question. And anything less would never be enough.

His eyes pinned her as his voice, deep and smooth, reached out. His fingers plucked at the strings as he ended the first chorus…each word branding itself on her heart.

She blinked. It was too much. Somehow… at some point Brody Hamilton had snuck past every single one of her defenses.

Somehow, in such a short space of time,

he'd become *everything*. And she had to stop it, and stop it now. She was leaving. She had to go back. She knew it and accepted it, as deeply as she understood exactly what it was she was feeling: she was completely in love with him.

The silk of his voice slid up her spine as she stood on the dance floor alone while couples circled slowly around her. Back to Marazur. Away from Brody. Away from Prairie Rose. Away.

And when his voice faded away with the last chord of the song it was just the two of them, caught in the moment, together though apart, and she understood exactly what it was her mother had meant when she'd spoken about Alexander.

Sometimes the choice was simply taken out of your hands. The thought cloaked her in fear.

She looked down at her feet, clad in his grandmother's shoes. There was no use in denying that she was connected to Prairie Rose now. But she couldn't do this. She couldn't set herself up to get her heart broken. She had seen her mother remain single her whole life because she'd given her heart to a man who didn't value it.

There'd been enough pain already. Enough dealing with her mother's death and promises she'd made. She had to leave. Leave the dance—surely Brody wouldn't walk out since he was hosting—and pack so she could get back to the life that was waiting for her. She'd dawdled enough.

The band had started up another song, a faster one, and people were crowding the floor once more. Lucy spun on her heel and headed straight for the doors and the stairs. The fairy tale—if it could be called a fairy tale—was over.

She was on the fourth step when he called out behind her.

"Lucy! Wait…"

She kept going, nearly frantic now in her need to get away. She dipped around a couple of teens who were lazily leaning against the railing. Hit the dirt at the bottom of the stairs and wished she were in boots instead of heels.

"Lucy…" His arm reached out and caught hers and her eyes slammed shut.

"Don't. Oh God, Brody, please don't."

She heard the plea in her voice and was helpless. If it took begging so be it.

"Let's get out of here," his voice rumbled

close to her ear, and her eyes snapped open as quickly as they'd shut.

"Are you kidding? I can't…we can't…what will…"

"Stop stammering. People are staring. Is that what you want?"

He pulled her halfway around so that she was staring up into his dark eyes.

"So help me God, Lucy, we need to talk about this, and I don't want to do it with an audience, but I will."

She nodded dumbly. He took her hand and led her away, his long strides forcing her to nearly jog in the shoes. She shivered even in the long sleeves; once the sun went down the air seemed to turn clear and cold.

Brody stopped several feet away from the shore of the pond. A few late-night ducks bobbed on the surface. The music from the dance echoed from behind them, punctuated with shouts and laughter from the partygoers inside. Instead of brash, the sounds had a misty quality about them.

"Brody, I—"

"Be quiet."

She faced him, her expression blank at his sharp tone. She didn't know what to say. His jaw ticked once, twice in the shadows and the unholy urge to touch the strong angle ran through her. "I just—"

"Dammit, Lucy, don't you ever listen?"

She opened her mouth to respond. And instead found it covered with his.

Oh. My. God. They were the only three words that she could find space for in her brain. His body was hard and unrelenting as he pulled her up against him. One hand captured her head just behind her ear, and his lips were a torturous delight as they assaulted hers. This was more demanding than any other kisses she'd experienced. His arms cinched her tightly in place and she gave up any hope of resisting. It was pointless. She wanted this as much as he did.

He planted his feet, and one hand pressed against her bottom, pulling her flush against his hips. Once she was there his hand slid up her ribs to cup a breast, and she moaned into his mouth.

"Let's go to the house," he suggested, the words strident with desire.

Lucy slid her lips away from his, closing her eyes. "I can't." The fact that she wanted to bit into her. "Please, Brody, just kiss me again."

He obliged with no resistance whatsoever,

but within moments it became clear to her he hadn't abandoned his initial objective.

She pushed him away, staggering backward. "No!" she gasped. "I can't. Oh, please, Brody, stop. I'm leaving on Monday. This would be a mistake."

"Why?" He had dropped his hold on her but was still close enough she could feel the heat from his body. It was too hard to think with him right in front of her, but this was one time she couldn't walk away.

"Because I'm leaving! Because we both know it won't go any further than this one night, and I'm not the sort of person that does that."

"And you think I am?"

She covered her lips with her hand for a moment, torn between simply wanting to give in and knowing she absolutely must not. "You're the one that suggested it, so I guess you must be."

"I haven't propositioned a woman in my life, Lucy Farnsworth. I've never asked a woman for sex."

She laughed harshly. He was making it easier after all. "You mean you don't *have* to ask, right? Well I'm not going to be some doe-eyed girl ready to fall all over herself to get in your bed!"

He stepped forward again, his lips a thin line and his jaw hard with anger. "Do you think that's what I want from you? Do you?"

She stepped up so they were toe-to-toe. "That's what you said! And seeing as my time left here can be counted in hours, what else am I supposed to think! What *do* you want from me, Brody?"

He spun away, took a few steps and stopped, his hands on his hips.

For long seconds he said nothing, while Lucy waited. She could tell he was trying to think of what to say, and for some reason she wanted to hear it. Wanted to hear him justify all the reasons. If she could only make him out to be as shallow as he sounded right now, it would be so much easier for her to leave.

The dance seemed a distant event. The cool nighttime breeze filtering through the trees was the only sound, wrapping itself around them. Lucy looked up. One by one, stars dotted the black night around them. She picked out the dipper, then the line that meant Orion and the *W* shape that meant Cassiopeia. A queen of unparalleled beauty. Lucy smiled sadly. She wasn't a queen. She wasn't even a princess, not really.

Brody turned back to her, his features softened slightly. "I'm sorry, Lucy. I got carried away. I got…"

"You got…?" She pinned him with the question.

"I got scared, all right? I find myself not wanting you to leave. There's something between us, and I'm not sure I'm ready for things to go back to normal around here after you go."

"What do you expect me to do, then?

She waited with bated breath. Would he ask her to stay, extend her time at Prairie Rose? Would he suggest something more than one night of passion? At this point she would grasp at anything. Anything to make this feeling of emptiness at the thought of going home go away.

"It's not what I want *from* you, Lucy, don't you get that? It's what I want *for* you."

She held her breath. This was madness. Utter and complete madness. He couldn't do this to her now. Now when she had no choice. She'd given her word. And he knew it. Why couldn't he be selfish? How could she want to be in two places at once? She closed her eyes, beyond confused, and with no idea how she was supposed to feel anymore.

"I know you have to go," he said softly. "I know it because it's what I'd do. I'd make the sacrifice to keep a promise."

"You already did."

"Yeah, I did. And I don't regret it, I don't. I love this ranch and I love my father, and loving them has never been a burden. It's the decisions, the responsibility that weighs heavy. But it's mine."

"I know that, Brody. I wish I could do something to help…"

"You have, Luce," he insisted, cutting her off. "More than you know. You have no idea what you have done for me. And I want you. You know it. Is that fair? No. But it's true. I want you tonight and you should know that before you walk away. You should know that you are wanted."

Tears clogged her throat. It was even more potent when he said it in that calm, rational voice. The beauty of being wanted sliced through her like a painful knife. Everything now was a double-edged sword, healing and hurting at the same time. "Brody, don't."

"If I don't say it now I never will. Lord, woman, how you got me to talk. Now I can't seem to stop. I need to say all the things now I would want to say on Monday when you're leaving and I won't be able to."

She fought back tears. This tender side of Brody called to her heart more than any other.

He cupped her cheek in his wide, rough hand. "I want you to be happy, and chase all your dreams, whatever they are and wherever they take you."

"I gave up on dreams a long time ago."

"I know, but you shouldn't have. And I wish I could carry your burdens for you. You've already had to carry so much, Lucy, with your mum dying. I don't want you to look back on your time here with regret but with a smile, because you changed so much for me. I want you to—"

He cleared his throat, and her heart cracked a little more.

"Life is full of choices, Lucy. The secret is picking the answer that means the most to you."

Lucy closed her eyes, unable to look in his earnest face. He couldn't possibly know how torn she was. She wanted to go home. She needed to see for herself what waited for her there. At the same time, she felt as if Prairie Rose was home.

"What if I don't know what that is?" Her voice was a whisper, carried on the westerly wind that was coming down from the mountains. "What then?"

"Then you look for the answer."

She waited. If he asked her now, she wasn't sure she could say no. If he asked her to stay with him she might just do it.

But he never asked.

And he'd never said he loved her, she realized, her heart sinking. In fact, she distinctly recalled him saying that he didn't believe in love anymore.

There really wasn't a choice to make. She couldn't stay and love a man who didn't love her back.

"Okay," she answered.

She took a step away, but his hand reached out and grabbed her wrist. "Don't go. Not now."

"I'm cold."

The chill was deepening as midnight approached. The stars hung close to the earth, and as she looked up, a satellite streaked across the sky, a perfectly curved path through the inky blackness.

"Then dance with me."

In the distance they heard the last dance

start playing up in the loft. They both turned their heads toward the wistful strains of "Let Me Call You Sweetheart" swaying toward them on the wind.

"Dance with me," he whispered, "one last time."

His wide hand was warm on her waist, her fingers enclosed in his as he started to lead her in a waltz, their feet making shushing noises in the soft grass. She closed her eyes, knowing that somehow a million stars shone down on them and she would have wished on each and every one if she could have figured out exactly what it was she wanted.

Their steps grew smaller and shorter, and within a few bars of the song she was pressed against the warm breadth of his chest, listening to his heart beat against her ear and knowing that at least once in her life she had experienced a completely perfect moment.

As the fiddle faded away, they were no longer dancing but simply swaying to the one-two-three rhythm of the song. Somewhere the band said good-night. Voices became louder as the barn cleared out and people made their way to their vehicles. And still she remained in his arms, unwilling to pull away. Because she knew when she did it would be the last time he ever held her.

Chapter Twelve

When Brody came downstairs, Lucy was already at the breakfast table. He took his seat opposite her, noting that she looked very prim and put together in a tidy white sweater. Her hair was up, too...not a corkscrew curl in sight. Instead it was pulled back and twisted up in something elegant. He wondered what had prompted her change from the usual jeans and T-shirts. Was it a reaction to their intimacy of last night? He smiled behind a finger.

After she'd left him at the pond he had known he'd said too much. The music and moonlight had made him all sentimental and…and needy. She'd finally run from him and he'd let her go, knowing that if he'd followed he probably would have said something he couldn't take back. And that *would* have been foolish. It was just the dance and her leaving that had made him speak the way he had.

She put a forkful of scrambled eggs on her fork and looked up at him. "Good morning."

"Good morning. How did you sleep?"

He winced at his own inanity. Good Lord. He was reduced to inquiring after her sleep now? He really was getting stupid over her. His own fault for being able to think about nothing other than her lying between the sheets last night, wondering if she was as restless as he.

"Fine."

Two spots of color erupted on her cheeks, and he knew she was lying. Good. Because he hadn't slept worth a damn, either. He'd tossed and turned, not sure if he wanted to go to her room and press his case or be completely irrational and ask her to stay on.

"Brody, I'm… I've decided to leave this morning. I'm going to drive up to Calgary and catch an earlier flight first thing tomorrow."

Leaving?

He turned his head toward the counter as the phone rang, but he let it. "Surely there's not that much of a rush." A tiny thread of panic slid through him. He wasn't ready for her to go. He'd thought he would have a whole day left. The phone stopped ringing; either whoever was on the other end had hung up or Mrs. Polcyk had answered it.

"One day sooner isn't going to make any difference. Our arrangements are all finalized. I don't need to be here any longer."

Her tone was cool. He stared at her for a long moment, but her gaze remained fixed on her plate. She'd given up eating, just pushed around a few fried potatoes for show.

"Stay, Lucy," he said suddenly. "Stay here."

Mrs. Polcyk came in from the office, her face suddenly drawn. "Lucy, phone's for you. It's *him*."

Brody watched as Lucy tore her gaze from his. He would have sworn from the way she was just looking at him that she was actually considering it. But the moment was lost as she turned to Mrs. P.

"Who, him?"

"King Alexander."

Lucy's fork hit her plate. "Tell him I'll call him back, that I'm busy for the moment."

"I already said you were at breakfast and he said...he said..." Uncharacteristically, the housekeeper faltered.

"He said?" Brody urged her, his brow furrowing. It wasn't like Mrs. P. to be flustered no matter who she was speaking to.

"He said to tell Princess Luciana he wished to speak to her right now."

Brody's gaze snapped to Lucy's. Her face had gone completely white. The words bounced around in his brain. Princess Luciana. Lucy Farnsworth. Princess Luciana.

She pushed back her chair, avoiding Brody's eyes which was just as well, because he couldn't keep the shock from his features. So many things raced through his mind he could hardly process them all; things she'd said or done over the past few weeks that suddenly made sense with a clarity so intense he couldn't believe he hadn't seen it before.

"Thank you, Mrs. P."

She extricated herself from the table gracefully and walked down the hall, with two pairs of eyes watching her every step.

"Did you know?" Brody asked Mrs. P. the moment the office door was closed.

"No."

Brody pushed his plate away, feeling sick. He'd made such a fool of himself. "Not a clue, Mrs. P?"

"None, Brody. I took her for who she was."

"Who she pretended to be, you mean."

Mrs. Polcyk didn't answer, just bustled through clearing plates. It was obvious no one was eating any more.

"What are you going to do?" she asked finally.

"What I should have done in the first place," he replied darkly. And he left the table and made the long walk down the hall to the office.

Lucy hung up the phone and rested her forehead on a hand. Her father hadn't known what he'd done, she was sure of it, and he'd wanted to talk to her now instead of two days from now because one of their mares had fallen and he wanted her input before making a decision.

Who knew her father would be so sentimental? His favorite mare had stepped in a hole and broken her leg. The vet had been called and was recommending they put her down, and Alexander had called her for her opinion. She sighed. Too bad she couldn't give him the answer he wanted. She knew the mare as a lovely, gentle soul. But the recovery for an older mare was long and difficult, and no matter what his attachment, simply not fair to the animal. She'd seconded the vet's opinion without a moment's hesitation. But it was never easy putting a horse down.

Brody strode into the room and she sighed, knowing exactly why he was there. "Can we do this later, please?" she asked, exhausted. She lifted her head from her hand and studied him with weary eyes. "I've just ordered a horse put down and I'm not up to an argument with you."

"That's too bad, because you're getting one."

Lucy inhaled deeply. "You're angry. I get that. But I'm leaving anyway."

"You can't possibly think that's enough of an explanation. Not after last night."

"Last night was a moment of whimsy."

"Then why can't you look at me when you say it?"

She forced her gaze upward again. His words were soft but his eyes were deadly.

And she knew they were going to have this out, here and now, anyway.

"I am Princess Luciana of Marazur," she conceded. "And that's nothing more than a technicality, because I'm also Lucy Farnsworth, daughter of Mary Ellen Farnsworth of Virginia. And that's who I was until a few months ago when my mother told me who my father was."

"I see." He bit the words out like they were distasteful, and Lucy was torn between wanting to yell at him and wanting him to understand.

"No, Brody, you don't. And I knew you wouldn't and that's why I didn't tell you."

"So you lied to me instead. You pretended to be someone you weren't."

"No!" She stood then, bracing her hands on the desk. "Don't you get it? I know who *Lucy* is. I don't know who Luciana is, and coming here I got a chance to just be *me* again! I got to be myself."

"You let me believe you were merely an employee for Navarro stables. When I asked you how you got hired, you said a friend-of-a-friend kind of thing. You lied right to my face. And that's inexcusable, Lucy."

"Of course it is," she scoffed, feeling the stirrings of anger. "You're perfect Brody Hamilton. The king of loyalty and honor and righteousness! The man who lost everything and came back better than ever. Tell me, Brody, did you make *any* mistakes along the way? Because you lost everything eight years ago and I lost it just this year and I have some catching up to do!"

"Don't." He made a slashing motion with his hand. "Don't turn this on me. You...we... I told you things, Lucy. I told you things about myself and this place because you made me trust you. And it was all based on a lie. You should have come clean with me."

Lucy came around the corner of the desk. "Don't you think I know that? Don't you think I felt guilty about it? Let me explain, Brody. Let me explain all of it, and then you can judge me however you want.

"My father met my mother when he was in Virginia, and they fell in love. Or so the story goes. He was crown prince but still very young, and recently widowed. He had two small sons at home. And she fell for him like a rock. According to my mum, he was rebelling a bit at being left a single father at such a young age. He flew her to Las Vegas and married her. And they spent a few weeks at Trembling Oak, without having told anyone what they'd done.

"He went back to Marazur with the plan to eventually tell his family that he had a new wife. But before he sent for her, the unthinkable happened. His father had a heart attack and died, and Alexander was forced to take over the throne. Imagine the PR nightmare of coronation with a new American bride at his side, fresh from a wedding at a Vegas chapel. My mum came from pretty humble beginnings, and that's putting it generously. It would have been an embarrassment.

"Oh, Mum was very generous in her opinion of him. She said that he didn't want to put her through that. That the pressures of being thrust into the position of queen and wife and stepmother were great and he wouldn't blame her for not wanting to take them on. And she didn't. Days before the coronation, their marriage was legally ended with no one the wiser."

"He didn't know about you?"

She shook her head. "No, and I knew nothing about him until the doctors said her cancer was inoperable. Even then she maintained that it had been her choice. That she hadn't wanted to be the cause of a scandal within a family that had already dealt with enough."

"So she made you promise."

"Yes, the same way you promised your father you'd look after Prairie Rose and Mrs. Polcyk. She made me promise to give Alexander a chance and I couldn't deny her, not when she was looking up at me with eyes so tired and in pain and yet with that little bit of hope. And like you, I couldn't break my word."

She licked her lips, catching her breath. At least he was listening now, and maybe understanding a little bit. "I went. And I've never felt more out of place in my life. My half brothers are carbon copies of Alexander— tall, dark, Mediterranean looks as opposed to my pale skin and red hair. They've grown up with titles and servants, and I'm used to a cup of tea in the kitchen. In the end Alexander didn't know what to do with me, so he sent me here. And I was determined to show him that I knew what I was doing." She gave a small sad smile. "Determined to show you, too. To show you both that Lucy Farnsworth is *somebody*. And so I kept my title a secret."

She closed her eyes for a moment, then opened them, walked across the floor past him and shut the door, enclosing them in the office.

"Let me ask you something. Would you have told me about Lisa if I hadn't let it out when we were arguing?"

At the set of his jaw, she knew the answer. "I thought so. I wasn't the only one keeping secrets."

"I never pretended to be someone I wasn't!" he said, stepping forward.

"It was still a secret. It was something close and painful to you that you didn't want to talk about. And the more you didn't talk about it, the more I knew how painful it must be to you, and I tried to respect your right to your own secrets. Because I had mine. And then once you told me about her, I knew I could never tell you who I was. You already thought I was like her. And you still do. I can see it in your eyes!"

"Well, she certainly pretended to be something she wasn't in order to get what she wanted."

That stung, especially since there was some truth in it. "Yes, but her motives were different from mine."

He turned away from her, but she could see the stubborn set of his jaw.

"Don't you think an ex-wife would have been a good thing to mention after we went to Wade's Butte? Why'd you do that, anyway? Why'd you take me to that place in particular? I know what it means to this family. It means something."

"I wanted to be with you, that's all."

Her heart surged at his words until he deflated it. "Only, I guess I didn't know who I was with after all."

His voice was so bitter it caused her physical pain. Her stomach cramped as she felt herself sinking deeper and deeper yet knowing they had to get it all out so they could leave it behind them. "And I felt horrible about that. Don't think I didn't feel guilty about not coming clean."

"Right," he said coldly.

She leaned back against the desk, needing its support. "I had to get away from Marazur. I was feeling stifled and angry, and I knew there were all these expectations of me that I hadn't asked for. And so, coming here was like a chance to just be me again. And I wanted you to deal with me as Lucy, not as the King's daughter. I wanted you to respect my knowledge and expertise and not think that I was a spoiled daughter sent on an errand.

"And I think somewhere along the way I earned that respect. I'm not sure that would have happened if you'd known who I was from the start. You would have seen the crown and not the person behind it."

She stopped. Brody said nothing, which she knew was as close to agreement as she was going to get.

"But then something else happened. We started having feelings. Or attraction. Whatever you want to call it. I felt at home here… with the ranch, and Mrs. Polcyk, and with you. And every moment, I knew I couldn't let myself get too attached because I was leaving. And that I had to cling to every single moment because it would be gone all too soon and I'd have to go back to being the princess again.

"And you kissed me. More than once, and held me like I was the most precious thing in the world. You told me about your father and the ranch and I knew more than ever that we are the same sort of people. Only, I knew if I told you the truth about who I was that would all be destroyed. So I kept quiet.

"And then it was too late. We got to a

point that you wouldn't ever understand. You danced with me under the stars. Do you have any idea what you've done to me, Brody? I wanted to hang on to that moment forever, even as the guilt about it all was eating me up inside! And I told myself the best thing was to pack and leave and make sure that this all stayed a beautiful memory."

"Luce—"

"Don't call me that," she snapped. "I can't bear it. Oh, I can't bear it, Brody."

Tears spurted into her eyes. Her heart was breaking bit by bit. "You opened your heart to me last night, but only as far as you would let it. Knowing that this was ending. So let it end. Please. Just let it end now before either of us gets hurt more than we already have."

"How could I possibly hurt you?" His hands burrowed into his pockets, and the lines of his face were taut with emotion. "You get to go back to your life."

She bit down on her lip. *But this is my life,* her heart cried. And he was pushing her out of it just as surely as she'd known he would. Already he wasn't seeing the woman she'd shown him over the past weeks but the facade her title provided. She loved him; that was a foregone conclusion. He didn't love her; that was fact, as well.

"I am not a machine," she whispered brokenly. "I have feelings. I have feelings for you. And I refuse to be like my mother. I understand now how her love for Alexander made it impossible for her to find someone else. The way that you're looking at me now hurts me. Leaving you and not seeing you again will hurt me, too. At least I'm honest enough to admit it."

"What's that supposed to mean?"

She looked him straight in the eyes. "You don't believe in love, anyway. So it doesn't matter."

His lips dropped open.

"You don't deny it. Can you even say the word?" He blinked, and his face became stony, hiding any expression. "And there go the shutters. I've known all along that you couldn't love me. So why would I spoil what little bit of you I could have by telling you about some title I've acquired that I didn't even want? You're the one who gets to go back to your life, not me. Well, maybe you were right last night. Maybe it's time I started looking for my life and deciding what it is I want."

She couldn't bear it any longer. If this was to be their goodbye, she had to get it over with before she lost herself completely. She could fall apart later when she was all alone. She had twenty-four whole hours before she was due on a plane and back to a life where privacy was a valuable commodity.

She darted past him and wrenched open the door. "If you cared anything about me, let me go now."

Half of her wanted him to let her escape and get away from the pain and resentment. The other half wanted him to stop her and tell her that it was all a big mistake.

But he didn't come after her, or call her name, or hold out a hand to stop her. Choking back the sobs, she fled upstairs to her room, grabbed her packed bags and dragged them out to the SUV.

She buckled her seat belt and stared at the dashboard where Bob usually sat, giving her directions in his monotone voice. She shoved the GPS in her purse and put the truck in gear.

She didn't need directions this time. She knew the way out perfectly well.

Lucy had been back several days already, but the memory of Brody and Prairie Rose was as fresh as if it had been only moments ago. She'd arrived tired and a bit broken, only to open her suitcase in her suite and find the shoebox with the navy shoes inside. Mrs. Polcyk. There had been a note too…a simple "She would have wanted you to have them." Touching them had reminded Lucy of dancing to the scrape of the fiddle, of that moment when Brody had teased her and she'd stomped on his toes. She'd cradled the shoes next to her and finally cried, releasing all the anguish she'd held in for the better part of two days. And when she'd finally stopped, she'd sent Mrs. Polcyk a short email thanking her and asking her forgiveness in not saying goodbye. Lucy knew the housekeeper understood.

The arrangements with Prairie Rose Ranch had been finalized through cool, businesslike emails, which Lucy had sent through the official Navarro Stables account, leaving her signature off them. If Alexander noticed, he said nothing. He'd been surprisingly undemanding since her return.

The only personal email to come her way from Alberta was from Mrs. P., who'd sent her a picture from the night of the barbecue. It was a candid shot of her with a piece of pie on a spatula and Brody standing just beyond her shoulder and both of them laughing. It reminded her of all the good things, before they'd been marred with the truth, and she'd printed it out. It sat in a frame now on the rosewood table next to her bed, a dried pink rose—the one he'd given her at Wade's Butte—tucked into the bottom corner of the frame. She sighed, reached out a finger and traced the outline of Brody's hat. Lord, she missed him so. Their harsh words at the end had done nothing to diminish her feelings.

A knock at her door made her look up, surprised to see her father's face peeking in. "Do you have a moment, Luciana?"

She no longer minded his use of the long form of her name—another thing that had changed. "Not at all. Come in."

He stepped inside, this man who was suddenly her father. He saw her hand on the photo and smiled softly. "You love him, don't you."

The question was so simple and intrinsically answered that a tear slipped out before she could prevent it. "Yes," she whispered. "Yes, I do."

"Oh, my daughter," he said softly, seeing her distress and taking quick steps to cross the room to take her in his arms. He was tall and strong and she let her head rest against his shoulder as she cried.

After a few minutes she pulled away, embarrassed that she'd acted in such a fashion. But he'd seemed to understand in a way she hadn't expected. He looked down into her eyes and she received another shock: they were very much like her own.

"I've been wondering if you'd ever see the resemblance," he said, squeezing her hand. "Come, let's sit. And you can tell me about this man who's broken your heart."

They sat on the edge of her bed. Lucy folded her hands and was unsure of how to begin. This was all so new.

"Do you know, the night before I left I saw Brody do this very thing. He held a girl in his arms because she'd had her heart broken by a boy, and I thought to myself how I'd never had someone like that in my life before."

"You do now," Alexander replied staunchly. "If you let me. Oh, Lucy, I want to be your father so much. I know it's been difficult. I thought perhaps Marazur was getting to be too hard for you so I sent you to Canada, thinking it would be good for you to get away. But I'm sorry. It seems all it's done is hurt you."

"No, it was something I needed to do," she said. She turned on the bed, sitting cross-legged before him, she in her everyday jeans and he in his customary tailored dark suit. His tie was slightly crooked, and she reached out to straighten it with a shy smile. "I blamed Mum and I said horrible things before she died, things I can never take back. After she was gone I put so much energy into resenting you for abandoning her that I never gave you a chance like she asked me to."

"You only reacted as anyone would, Lucy, you can't blame yourself for being human. You must know we thought we were doing the right thing," Alexander said, looking at his hands. "I loved your mother. It was a lot to ask of her, to take on a country and a husband and children who were still raw from losing a parent. If I'd known about you, though, I would have found a way. I swear to you, I would have. But then… I never wanted her to resent the choice she'd made. I never wanted our love to be a burden."

Lucy remembered something Brody had said their last night together, in the moonlight by the pond. She said, "Love isn't a burden. Perhaps a responsibility, but never a burden."

"How did you get so wise?" Her father smiled and laid a hand along her curls.

"Someone told me that once," she whispered.

"And?"

"And then he found out that I wasn't Lucy Farnsworth but Luciana, Princess of Marazur."

Understanding flickered in his eyes. "That's my fault, isn't it."

"No, it's not. It's just the way it is." She sighed. "I should have been honest in the beginning and told him who I was. Or at least told him, once it was clear there was something between us. I was so bent on pretending the princess side of me didn't exist that I didn't trust him." She looked up at him, into the eyes so like her own. "Oh, Papa, I was so wrong."

Alexander stood up abruptly and walked to the window. Lucy's eyes followed him and saw him raise a hand to his face, swiping it over his mouth and chin. "I beg your pardon," he said, trying for control but failing as the emotion crept into his voice. "I wasn't expecting that."

He turned back to her. "We...that means Raoul and Diego and I...we want you to be a part of this family. Please believe that, Lucy."

"I do. I only needed to realize it, and my time away helped me to see that what I believed to be expectations were really just you trying to make me feel like I belonged." She went to him and took his hands in hers. "I would very much like to be your daughter. In any capacity you wish."

The acceptance was bittersweet. But she had the choice now, and if she couldn't have Brody she could at least choose to have a family.

"Of course I wish it. I only kept it quiet because I didn't think you wanted it to be made public."

"I thought maybe you didn't want the details of your marriage to my mother to come out."

"Why, when the result is so beautiful?" he asked, and she smiled.

"What do I have to do?"

His eyes lit. "My darling, you just need to be yourself. And what about Mr. Hamilton?"

Lucy turned around and looked at the picture. "It doesn't matter. He doesn't love me."

She turned back and smiled up at her father. "I need to move forward. Let's do it."

Alexander pressed a kiss to her forehead. "I think it's time the world met Luciana Navarro, Princess of Marazur. What do you think?"

Chapter Thirteen

Lucy looked at her reflection in the cheval mirror. The last time she'd done so she'd been wearing a vintage skirt and western blouse getting ready for a barn dance. Now she was wearing a gown and getting ready for a ball. Her ball.

She plucked at the filmy overskirt with her fingers, feeling the fine stitching of blue flowers and green leaves against the white background. It was a fairy dress, strapless and white and flowing to the floor in dreamy folds. Alexander's idea of combining her introduction with her birthday was lovely... lending a personal touch to a formal occasion.

And she wasn't nervous. But she wasn't completely happy, either.

There was another knock on the door; maids had been coming and going most of the day. "Come in," she called, but it was her half brother, Raoul, who came in, the crown prince himself, looking very dashing in tuxedo and sash.

"May I?"

"Of course."

She liked Raoul, even if sometimes they were still reserved with each other. She was okay with that. At least she knew when he said something, he genuinely meant it. He held out a velvet box. "Happy birthday."

She took the box from his hands. "Should I open it now?"

"Please."

She put it down on the table and with satin gloved hands, flipped the lid open with a stiff creak. Inside was nestled a perfect diamond-studded tiara.

"It was Mother's," he said gently. "She wore it at their wedding ball."

She understood what the gesture meant. "Oh, Raoul, it's lovely, but I shouldn't."

"We want you to, Lucy. You're a part of this family now." His voice was thick, and he cleared his throat. "Besides," he added dryly, "this means Diego will have to stop pestering Papa for a baby sister to aggravate."

She laughed. Diego was twenty-six and incorrigible, far more easygoing than the serious Raoul.

"Will you help me put it on?"

He took the slender tiara from her fingers and settled it atop her fiery ringlets. "I'm not sure which is brighter, little sister. The diamonds or your hair."

She hugged him impetuously. "Thank you, Raoul."

He set her back and bowed. "I know Papa has the first dance, but I'd be honored if you'd dance with me tonight, Lucy."

"Of course."

When he was gone, she sat on the bed, her hand pressed against the nerves in her stomach. There was only one thing missing now, and that was Brody and Prairie Rose. But she couldn't have both. Or could she?

She stared at the satin slippers waiting on her spread, a smile creeping up her lips. She went to her closet and instead took out the navy shoes, slipping them on her feet. "Well, Grandma Hamilton, you're going to the ball tonight," she murmured, suddenly feeling completely put together.

Alexander met her at her door and escorted her down the long curving stairs to the foyer and then to the doors of the ballroom. "Happy birthday, Luciana," he murmured, and then nodded at the footmen. The doors swung open and she entered on his arm, everything in a haze, including being announced as Luciana Navarro, Princess of Marazur.

Never had she been in such a place. Liveried servants circulated among the guests, and Lucy, her father and brothers formed an official receiving line where she could be properly—and personally—introduced. It was very surreal, being addressed as Princess Luciana or Your Highness. She smiled, thinking she should really just be called "Lucy of the Stables." But then her father squeezed her elbow and smiled at her and she was suddenly glad she had him there at her side. If her thoughts drifted to Brody now and then, that was okay. One didn't get over a broken heart in a few weeks.

There was cake, a frothy concoction of vanilla fluff and real flowers, and enough champagne to float the entire island of Marazur. Lucy was holding a glass when Alexander touched her elbow and said, "We are ready to start the dancing."

He cued the orchestra and held out his hand. She took it in her gloved one and bit down on her lip at the look in his eyes. And when he pulled her into his arms and guided her steps, she leaned ahead and whispered, "Thank you, Papa," in his ear.

At the end of that dance she was paired off with Raoul, who complimented her on her dancing, and then Diego, who made a joke about her wild hair and the tiara, which caused her to snort in a most unladylike way. Grandma's shoes made several more turns with the heads of influential families in Europe before she was passed back to Alexander once more.

"Are you tired?" he asked, as their waltz was nearly over.

"A little."

"And your feet?"

She smiled. "I've been on them all night."

His smile broadened suddenly. "Do you think they can manage one more dance?"

"I suppose, but why..."

"Your birthday present has just arrived."

He turned her a half turn toward the doors.

Brody.

Everything in her slammed to her chest. He was here. In Marazur. Standing twenty feet away from her in a tuxedo, his hat nowhere to be found, his dark eyes glittering at her dangerously. Instead of a bowtie, he wore a bolo.

To her, he was perfect.

Alexander still held one shaking, gloved hand. "When there is a choice to be made, my darling, one should always choose love." And he let her go, stepped back.

Everything in her wanted to race across the floor and fling herself into his arms. Yet she held herself back and waited, heart pounding, as he took step after torturous step until he was before her, in the middle of the ballroom, with three hundred pairs of eyes on them.

And when the orchestra started playing "Let Me Call You Sweetheart," he took her in his arms without a word and turned her around the floor.

Oh glorious, glorious day. Her heart swelled to bursting, she reveled in the feeling of his hand at her waist, the way his fingers curled around hers and the heat of his body as he led her across the floor in an effortless waltz. She looked into his eyes, unable to look away from what she saw there.

"This was what was missing," she whispered, as he executed a sweeping turn.

"What?"

"You. Just you."

His eyes dropped to her lips for the tiniest of seconds before moving back up again.

She smiled, suddenly so happy she thought she might explode. "I'm wearing your grandmother's shoes," she confided.

"I wondered why you danced so well."

"Mrs. P. gave them to me."

"She told me."

"Do you two have any secrets?"

He finally smiled, a devilish curve that delighted her. "A few. Now be quiet and dance."

By the time the final bars were played, they were both grinning like fools. He stepped back and executed a perfect bow. And with one raised eyebrow, she dropped into a deep, delectable curtsy, her skirts billowing out like a white and blue cloud around her.

He held out his hand and she took it, and he led her to the balcony.

They walked to the balustrade, shrouded in darkness. Brody lifted his nose to the breeze. "It smells different here. Feels different."

"It's the ocean. And…well, it's Europe."

She laughed. It faded away into the perfumed evening. "I had no idea you were coming."

"His Highness invited me."

"So I gather."

She could almost hear Brody's smile in the dark. "That man's got a tone that's as effective as any shotgun."

She couldn't help it, she burst out laughing. The picture of Alexander in his designer suit and a twelve-gauge in his hand tickled her funny bone. "He couldn't have been that bad."

"Pardon me, but it was like a long-distance Spanish inquisition."

She covered her mouth with a hand. "What did he say?"

His response echoed in the darkness. "Nothing I didn't already know."

"Like?"

He came to her, took her hand in his and tilted her chin up with a finger. "Like I was a damned fool."

"Well, shoot," she whispered. "I could have told him that."

"And to be honest, when he called I was already making arrangements. I had to come." The pad of his thumb touched the crest of her cheekbone. "I had to make things right. All

I could think of on the plane was what if I had blown it?"

He smiled at her, touched the tip of her nose with his finger. "Do you know how beautiful you look tonight?"

"It took several people all day to accomplish this."

"Don't do that," he ordered. "Don't. You are beautiful. Almost as beautiful as you were when you turned the corner at the soddy that afternoon."

She was stunned. Way back then? She'd been dirty and grubby from riding. "I had on old jeans and a T-shirt and was getting a sunburn."

"And you were the prettiest thing I'd ever seen."

"Oh, Brody…"

"Gorgeous," he continued. "My prairie rose. And not like the roses from the shop. Simpler. Beautiful, strong and resilient."

She pressed a gloved hand to her lips, overwhelmed. "You really mean that."

"Of course I do. I'm sorry," he said firmly. "I'm sorry for laying all the blame on you. I was so angry that morning, and felt so foolish, and everything you said was completely right and I was too proud to see it. Too proud and too afraid."

"I don't know what to say."

The sea breeze ruffled his hair, carrying the perfume of the gardens up to them from below. "You had your say," he replied. "And now I want to have mine. And what I have to say is this. It was a mistake for me to let you walk away, Lucy Farnsworth. Or Princess Luciana or whatever you want me to call you."

Her smile was tremulous as she cupped his jaw with her satin-clad hand. "Sweetheart would do nicely."

"Sweetheart."

"I'm sorry, Brody, for everything that happened at the ranch. I never wanted to hurt you."

"I know that now."

The sounds of the orchestra wafted out on the breeze and Lucy laughed lightly. "I don't know what it is about us and dances, but we always seem to be 'out here' when everyone else is 'in there.'"

"If we were in there I couldn't do this." He traced her lips with a finger, and then replaced it with his mouth.

Nothing in the world had ever felt so right

as the feel of his mouth against hers. It made every cell in her want to weep with welcoming. For a few blissful moments Marazur didn't matter. Prairie Rose didn't matter. Home was being held in Brody Hamilton's arms and being kissed as if she was the most cherished woman in the world.

When their lips parted, he rested his forehead on hers for a moment, the warmth of his breath fluttering over her skin and raising the fine hairs everywhere on her body.

He stepped back and looked at her in the moonlight. "Look at you," he murmured, his eyes dark and wide. "Like an angel. Or a princess." He smiled then, that lopsided one that made him half rogue, half prince charming. "You even have the tiara."

Her fingers flew to it out of instinct. "Raoul gave it to me today. My half brother," she explained. "It was his mother's."

"You've found a family here after all."

"Yes, I have. Things have changed... Papa has turned out to be so kind, and even the boys..." She chuckled. "They hate being called boys. They've accepted me as their sister. You helped me to see that it was me who stood in the way of having a family. I had so much resentment. And now...now I have a family who loves me. Who supports me. It's all quite overwhelming."

"You're happy."

There was an edge to the words, and she thought she understood why. "I'm contented, and that's more than I ever expected."

To her surprise, Brody walked away, moving to stand next to a potted tree, resting his elbows on the stone railing and looking out over the courtyard.

"I'm at a royal palace in Europe."

She smiled, though she knew something was off. "It's kind of surreal, isn't it."

"I told myself it was better to let you go, to let you find your own way...so things could return to the way they had been. Now when I look at you, I can't help but think that might have been right then. You're not the Lucy I knew—not tonight—and yet you are. I don't quite know what to make of it all."

"How about if you just tell me what you want?"

He tucked his hands into his pockets. She realized he did that when he was particularly nervous, and she couldn't help the tiny smile that touched her lips.

"I look at you, Lucy, and I still see that girl standing up to me about Pretty's hoof. I see the girl I kissed out at Wade's Butte and the one I wanted to make love to the night of the dance. And I don't know how that's possible, because I'm still not sure she exists. And yet…everything you said about Lisa that morning was true. And I realized that deep down I think we *are* the same sort of people. We want the same thing…someone to love us even though we're determined not to let them.…

"And I love you, Lucy. Whether or not anything comes of it, I have to tell you. I love you. And I'm not afraid of it anymore. I'm only afraid you don't love me back."

Finally Lucy did what she'd been wanting to do since she'd seen him standing, waiting for her. She launched herself into his arms and wrapped her arms around his neck.

"Of course I love you! Why else do you think I've been tied up in knots for the last month and a half!"

Tears sparkled in her eyes as she slid down his chest, her wrists still anchored firmly around his neck. "I thought you didn't believe in love."

"I didn't. But you know what? Something funny happened. I believed in you."

"You didn't."

He gripped her waist tighter. "Yes, I did. Which is why when I found out the truth, I felt like the rug had been pulled out from beneath me."

"I've loved you since that afternoon at Wade's Butte when you told me about your family."

He pushed her back a little, his hands on her hips. "Way back then?"

She nodded. "Way back then. And I knew if I confessed you'd hate me, and I couldn't bear the thought of it. And that look in your eyes the morning I left... I knew you despised me and it broke my heart."

"I never want to hurt you like that again."

For long moments he held her in his arms. But as the evening chilled, reality crept in. "There are still logistics to consider."

Lucy heard the tone in his voice, and something heavy settled in the pit of her stomach. He couldn't have come all this way just to leave again, could he? But then she thought of her parents. They had loved each other, too, but their lives were so different that they hadn't found a way to reconcile them.

"What do we do now?" she whispered. If he were leaving again, she wanted to have this conversation and get it over with. "I know you would never leave the ranch. And I couldn't ask you to."

"You're still a princess and I'm still a rancher. Worlds apart."

Lucy angled her head and looked up at him. "Not really. If we were, I wouldn't have been at Prairie Rose in the first place."

His black eyes were piercing as he looked down at her. "True."

Another few moments, and Lucy dipped her chin.

"And you've found a family who loves you and wants you, right here. It wouldn't be fair to ask you to leave them."

Again silence.

"And there's the matter of the promises we made."

"Yes," she whispered.

Laughter and voices came from inside, and silence reigned on the terrace.

Then Lucy's voice broke the silence, and she surprised herself at the strength in it. "I also have a father whose last piece of advice was that when faced with a choice, I should follow my heart."

"Good advice," Brody replied, his voice deeply intimate in the darkness.

"Brody, I…"

"No, Lucy, it's my turn."

He stood back, and her heart turned over as he knelt on one knee. Torturously, one by one, he pulled at the fingers of her left glove until they were all loosened, and then pulled the long satin cuff off her arm. He held it in one hand while the other took a ring from his jacket pocket, slipping it over her fourth finger. "Marry me, Lucy. I think you're going to *have* to marry me because I'm pretty sure I can't do without you."

She tugged on his hand and he rose, and she cupped his face in her hands. "What *took* you so long!" Her laugh danced off the stone walls of the palace. "Yes, I'll marry you! Didn't I already tell you Prairie Rose felt like home to me? And home is where *you* are, Brody. Nowhere else. I was just waiting for you to ask!"

"But your family here…"

"Will be my family here. Think of the marvelous vacations we'll have. Not to mention being allied with one of the premier stables in Europe."

"There is that."

She leaned up and kissed him hard on the mouth. "We should tell Papa. He'll be so pleased." She tugged on his hand, pulling him toward the French doors that led to the ballroom.

He planted his feet and stopped her progress. "Lucy, you know that's not why I asked, right?"

"Of course I know." She tugged off her other glove and laid them both on the edge of a planter filled with flowers. "I said I didn't want to be like my mother, and that's true. She gave up on the man she loved. And that's one thing I promise I'll never, ever do."

He swung her up in his arms and spun her around, and her tiara tumbled off and danced across the stone floor as he kissed her. She thought there was a very good chance she would never, ever get tired of kissing him back.

Finally he put her down and bent to retrieve her tiara. "Let's put this back on, Princess Luciana." He tucked it gently into the strands of hair that still remained pulled back in tiny diamond clips. Then he stood back and looked at her.

"For now," she whispered, unable to tear her gaze away from the admiration she saw in his eyes. "Where I'm headed I won't have need of it." She reached up and cupped his jaw, her ring sparkling in the moonlight. "I'll only need you."

He turned his head and kissed her palm, the heat of his breath warming her all over. "We should go in," he murmured, and she thought she heard a trace of reluctance in his voice. But there would be time to be alone later. Forever.

"I think this is one of the best demonstrations of multitasking I've ever seen," Lucy said, squeezing his hand as they reached the doors, preparing to enter together. "Just think…tonight will always be known as my coming out, my birthday and my engagement ball!"

* * * * *

WESTERN WP PROMISES

YES! Please send me **The Western Promises Collection** in Larger Print. This collection begins with 3 FREE books and 2 FREE gifts (gifts valued at approx. $14.00 retail) in the first shipment, along with the other first 4 books from the collection! If I do not cancel, I will receive 8 monthly shipments until I have the entire 51-book Western Promises collection. I will receive 2 or 3 FREE books in each shipment and I will pay just $4.99 US/ $5.89 CDN for each of the other four books in each shipment, plus $2.99 for shipping and handling per shipment. *If I decide to keep the entire collection, I'll have paid for only 32 books, because 19 books are FREE! I understand that accepting the 3 free books and gifts places me under no obligation to buy anything. I can always return a shipment and cancel at any time. My free books and gifts are mine to keep no matter what I decide.

272 HCN 3070 472 HCN 3070

Name	(PLEASE PRINT)	
Address		Apt. #
City	State/Prov.	Zip/Postal Code

Signature (if under 18, a parent or guardian must sign)

Mail to the **Reader Service**:

IN U.S.A.: P.O. Box 1867, Buffalo, NY 14240-1867
IN CANADA: P.O. Box 609, Fort Erie, Ontario L2A 5X3

* Terms and prices subject to change without notice. Prices do not include applicable taxes. Sales tax applicable in N.Y. Canadian residents will be charged applicable taxes. This offer is limited to one order per household. All orders subject to approval. Credit or debit balances in a customer's account(s) may be offset by any other outstanding balance owed by or to the customer. Please allow 4 to 6 weeks for delivery. Offer available while quantities last. Offer not available to Quebec residents.

WPBPA16R

REQUEST YOUR FREE BOOKS!

2 FREE NOVELS PLUS 2 FREE GIFTS!

H HARLEQUIN®

SPECIAL EDITION

Life, Love & Family

REQUEST YOUR FREE BOOKS!
2 FREE NOVELS PLUS 2 FREE GIFTS!

HARLEQUIN®

American Romance®

LOVE, HOME & HAPPINESS

HAR15